THE SELFLESS ACT

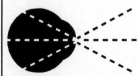

This Large Print Book carries the
Seal of Approval of N.A.V.H.

THE AMISH MILLIONAIRE, BOOK 6

THE SELFLESS ACT

WANDA E. BRUNSTETTER & JEAN BRUNSTETTER

THORNDIKE PRESS
A part of Gale, Cengage Learning

GALE
CENGAGE Learning·

Farmington Hills, Mich • San Francisco • New York • Waterville, Maine
Meriden, Conn • Mason, Ohio • Chicago

GALE
CENGAGE Learning®

LIBRARY OF CONGRESS CATALOGING-IN-PUBLICATION DATA

Names: Brunstetter, Wanda E., author. | Brunstetter, Jean, author.
Title: The selfless act / by Wanda E. Brunstetter & Jean Brunstetter.
Description: Large print edition. | Waterville, Maine : Thorndike Press, 2016. | Series: The Amish millionaire ; #6 | Series: Thorndike Press large print Christian fiction
Identifiers: LCCN 2016029452 | ISBN 9781410488022 (hardcover) | ISBN 1410488020 (hardcover)
Subjects: LCSH: Amish—Pennsylvania—Lancaster County—Fiction. | Large type books. | GSAFD: Christian fiction.
Classification: LCC PS3602.R864 S45 2016 | DDC 813/.6—dc23
LC record available at https://lccn.loc.gov/2016029452

Published in 2016 by arrangement with Barbour Publishing, Inc.

Printed in Mexico
1 2 3 4 5 6 7 20 19 18 17 16

THE SELFLESS ACT

CHAPTER 1

Millersburg, Ohio

Joel smiled, glancing at the box full of red- and green-wrapped packages on the passenger seat beside him. He'd bought these gifts for his sisters, their husbands, and Aunt Verna and Uncle Lester. More packages in the back of his truck waited for his nieces and nephews. He hoped his generosity in bringing Christmas presents would be well-received.

What could be more selfless than

buying Christmas gifts for seventeen family members when I'm short on money? he thought. Thankfully, Joel had been able to borrow some money from his buddy Tom Hunter. But of course that meant one more obligation to pay. Joel still hadn't gotten all his subcontractors paid from jobs they'd done for him several months ago. He wondered if he'd ever be debt free.

"Should be doing more than fine if I ever get my share of Dad's will," he mumbled, turning in the direction of his sister Elsie's house, where he'd been invited for Christmas dinner. If Elsie, Arlene, Doris, and Aunt Verna thought the gifts he'd brought for everyone qualified as a selfless act, before the day was out, he might get to open the envelope Dad had left for him.

Guiding his truck onto the back country road leading to Elsie and John's place, Joel's hands began to sweat. *What if Aunt Verna thinks the gifts I bought are superficial and not a selfless act? She does have the final say. And until she's convinced I've committed a selfless act, I'm not getting any of Dad's money.*

When Joel had apologized to his ex-girlfriend Anna for hurting her during their breakup more than seven years ago, his aunt hadn't seen it as a heartfelt, much less selfless deed. Aunt Verna could be tough like Joel's dad — stubborn, too. When she made up her mind about something, there was no changing it. Joel needed to keep on her good side. If he said enough nice things to his aunt today and she liked the gifts he'd bought everyone, it might help his cause.

Pulling into Elsie's driveway, Joel slammed on the brakes and did a double-take. "Oh, no! What happened?"

Joel undid his seatbelt and hopped out of the truck. He almost pinched himself to see if he was in the middle of a nightmare. The smell of burned wood and ash made him cough. His sister's house was gone — burned to the ground.

Joel's heart hammered in his chest as he got back in his truck and turned it around. *I need to find Elsie — see if everyone's okay. Maybe they're at Arlene's. If not, then she may know why their house caught fire and where they're staying.*

Farmerstown, Ohio

After Joel pulled up to the barn by Arlene and Larry's house, he turned off the engine, hopped out, and raced up the porch steps. He'd only knocked once when the door opened and Doug stuck his head out.

"Where's your mother? I need to talk to her right away."

"She and my *daed* are at the hospital with Scott." Doug stared up at him with a curious expression.

Joel's mouth hung slightly open. "What's wrong with your brother?"

He pushed his hands deep into his pockets.

Doug opened the door wider and stepped aside. "You look cold. You'd better come in, and we'll tell you about it."

The icy air cut through Joel's boots, so he stomped the snow off his feet and did as the boy suggested. Anxious to know why Scott and his parents were at the hospital, Joel also wanted to find out if anyone knew about the fire that had destroyed his eldest sister's house. It didn't take long for him to ask, because Elsie and John, along with Uncle Lester and Aunt Verna, were seated on the living-room sofa. The children — Martha, Mary, Hope, and Lillian — sat on the floor near the fireplace, while Glen and Blaine occupied the two recliners. The somber expressions on what should have been a joyous Christmas afternoon revealed the depth of everyone's sorrow.

Joel stood in front of the couch, looking down at them. He opened his mouth, but at first, nothing came out. He wasn't sure what to say. "I . . . uh . . . just came from Millersburg and was stunned when I saw what little remains of your house. What happened, Elsie? Was anyone hurt?"

"No." John's shoulders slumped. "We were here last night, having supper with the rest of the family, and soon after Scott was taken to the hospital, we headed for home."

He paused, rubbing his hand down one side of his bearded face. "When we got there and saw our house engulfed in flames, I ran to the phone shack and called for help."

"Unfortunately, by the time the fire trucks came, our house was gone." Elsie's chin trembled. "We have nothing left, Joel. Only the clothes on our back." She dabbed at her tear-filled eyes with a tissue.

"And the barn," John added. "Fortunately, it's far enough from the house so it didn't catch fire from any sparks."

"Of course, we can't live in the barn." Elsie's voice sounded strained, and she sniffed, rubbing her nose with the tissue. "We don't know how long it'll be before we can afford to rebuild."

"You'd best wait till spring, when the weather is warmer," Uncle Lester interjected. "By then, maybe a benefit auction can take place to help with your expenses."

Aunt Verna nodded and clasped Elsie's hand. "We're thankful none of you were inside when the fire started. Material possessions can be replaced, but lives cannot."

Material possessions can't be replaced if you don't have money to replace them, Joel was tempted to retort. Knowing his sister and aunt wouldn't appreciate his thoughts, he kept them to himself. "I'm sorry for your loss." He shifted his weight from one foot to the other. "Do you know how the fire got started?"

John shook his head. "Elsie's sure she didn't leave the stove on, and we didn't have a fire in the fireplace. I thought all the gas lamps were out before we left to come here to celebrate Christmas Eve, but I may have carelessly forgotten to turn one off."

Joel rubbed the heel of his palm against his chest as he tried to calm his nerves. His sister and brother-in-law's situation was tragic, but there was nothing he could do to help them out. Given his own financial issues, he didn't have any extra cash to give.

He sank into the rocking chair across from them, and Doug knelt on the floor beside him. "Do ya wanna hear about Scott now?" the boy asked, looking up at Joel.

"Yes, I do." Joel focused his attention on Doug.

"He complained of a bellyache last night and started throwin' up. So Dad called a driver, and they took him to the hospital."

"It sounds like the flu to me. Why would they take him to the hospital for that?"

"It wasn't the flu." Elsie's lips compressed. "Scott was in so much pain he couldn't even walk. When they got to the hospital, they found out his appendix had ruptured."

"Wow! Is he gonna be okay?" Joel rubbed the bridge of his nose.

"I spoke with Arlene on the phone after Scott came out of surgery. He seemed to be doing all right, but the doctor is worried about infection from the poison that was spread when it ruptured." Elsie sighed. "If I could be at the hospital right now, I'd know more. Sitting here, thinking about the fire and worrying about Scott is taking its toll on me." She paused to wipe the tears on her cheeks with another tissue. "This has not been a good Christmas for the *kinner* or us adults."

"Where's Doris? Does she know about all this?" Joel asked.

"I called and left a message on their answering machine this morning," John replied. "I'm sure once they hear the news they'll come over right away. I left a message for you, too, Joel, but your mailbox was full."

"Yeah, sorry about that. I need to delete some messages." Joel stood up and tightened his fists. "I want to find out how Scott's doing." He looked at Elsie. "Do you know what hospital they took him to?"

"Union, in Dover." Elsie stood, too. "Would you mind if I go with you? I'm sure Arlene could use some support."

"That's fine. I have a box of Christmas presents for everyone out in the truck. I'll bring them inside, and as soon as you're ready to go, we can be on our way."

Berlin, Ohio
Using one crutch under her arm for support, Doris stood at the

stove, scrambling eggs. She'd been able to do a few more things on her own lately and wanted to have breakfast ready for Brian when he came in from doing chores.

She finished the eggs and was about to put them in the oven to keep warm, when Brian entered the kitchen. His grim expression let Doris know something was amiss. "What's wrong? You look *umgerennt.*"

"I am upset, and you will be too when you hear this news." He removed his knitted cap and hung it on a wall peg, then took a seat at the table, motioning for Doris to do the same.

"What is it, Brian? You're scaring me." She hobbled across the room and lowered herself into the chair across from him.

"I stopped at the phone shack to check for messages and found one from John." Deep wrinkles formed across Brian's forehead. "Their house caught fire last night. They lost everything."

Doris's spine stiffened. She clutched the edge of the table. "*Ach,* that's *baremlich*! Was anyone hurt?"

"No, but there's nothing left of the house. John said they spent last night at Arlene and Larry's. I'm guessing that's where they still are."

"We ought to be with them. They need our support right now." Doris grabbed her crutch and started to stand.

"Let's eat breakfast first."

"I . . . I don't think I can." She felt as if a lump was stuck in her throat. "I feel sick about this."

"Same here." Brian drew in a deep breath. "There's more, Doris."

"Wh–what do you mean?"

"When Larry and Arlene took Scott to the hospital last night, they found out his appendix had ruptured."

"Oh, no!" She covered her mouth and fell back in her chair, dropping her crutch to the floor. *Lord, why are so many terrible things happening to our family?* she prayed. *How much more can we take?*

Dover, Ohio

Elsie stood in the hospital waiting room, sobbing as she hugged her sister. "What a horrible Christmas this has turned out to be for all of us."

Arlene's tears wet Elsie's dress as she gently patted her back. "I'm so sorry to hear of your loss. I can't imagine how it must feel to have lost your home and everything in it."

"It's a small thing compared to the loss of a loved one. I hope and pray Scott's going to be okay."

"Same here." Joel stepped up to them. "The little guy doesn't deserve this."

"Loss and illness are hard," Larry said. "But with God's help and with support from each other, we'll all get through this."

"I brought him a gift, but it's at your house. Guess I can give it to him when he gets home." Joel glanced down the hall. "I don't suppose he's up to company yet."

Larry shook his head. "He's sleeping and needs his rest. Let's sit down and visit while we're waiting for him to wake up."

Arlene drew in her bottom lip. "I'll sit a few minutes, but then I'm going back to his room. I want to be there when he wakes up."

Elsie and Arlene sat beside each other while the men pulled up chairs facing them.

"You're welcome to stay at our house for as long as you like."

Arlene lightly stroked Elsie's forearm as she spoke in a quiet tone. "But it might work better for your family if you moved into Dad's old place until you're able to rebuild. There's more room there, and you can all spread out."

"True, but Aunt Verna and Uncle Lester are staying there now, as well as Glen." Elsie massaged the back of her neck, contemplating things. "Once they return to their home in Burton, John and I can take the downstairs bedroom, which would free one of the upstairs rooms so Blaine and Glen wouldn't have to share." It was difficult to look at the positives right now, but bemoaning their situation wouldn't change a thing. They would have to make the best of their situation and be grateful they had a warm place to stay.

Joel glanced at his cell phone and scratched his jaw. "The Weather Channel has issued a warning for a snowstorm that will hit the area within the next hour." He turned to Elsie. "I think we should go now, before the roads get real bad, or we could end up stuck here overnight."

"You two go ahead. I'm not going anywhere until I'm sure Scott's out of danger," Arlene was quick to say. "Larry and I spent last night here, and we'll stay as long as needed."

"That's right," her husband agreed.

Arlene offered Elsie a tired-looking smile as she leaned her back against the chair. "*Danki* for bringing Larry and me a change of clothes."

"You're welcome. I feel bad you'll have to spend another night trying to sleep in a chair, when you ought to be home in your own bed."

"We'll be okay." Larry stood. "I'm going to the vending machine to get some coffee. Would anyone else like some?" He looked at Joel. "Maybe you'd like a cup for the road."

"No, that's okay. Vending machine coffee's not for me. I like mine fresh."

Elsie made no comment as she slipped on her outer garments. She wished she could stay at the hospital with Arlene, but John and the children were waiting for her. After the trauma they'd all been through on Christmas Eve, her place was with them.

CHAPTER 2

Charm, Ohio

"*Hallich Neiyaahr,* Mama!" Hope stepped up to Elsie and gave her a hug.

"Happy New Year to you, too." Returning the hug, and forcing a smile, Elsie patted her youngest daughter's head. It was good for the children to be optimistic, but Elsie felt as though her world had been turned upside down. These were the times when being a parent and trying to hold things together could be daunting. She was thankful to be staying in Dad's old house but missed her own place, where she and John started their life together nearly twenty-two years ago. So many memories had been made there — all gone up in smoke. At least none of the animals had been affected by the fire. They'd been brought over to Dad's place, but with his horses taking up most of the stalls in the barn, they had to do a bit of shifting to make room.

"Are we gonna do anything special today?" Hope looked up at Elsie with expectancy.

"I don't think so." Elsie yawned and sat down in her dad's recliner. "I'm feeling kind of *mied* this morning."

"I know why you're tired," John said when he entered the living room. "You got up at the crack of dawn." He took a seat in the chair beside her as Hope scampered out of the room.

Elsie yawned a second time, stretching her arms over her head. "I'm used to our queen-size mattress and couldn't sleep any longer in that small bed."

"Lester and I can move upstairs and let you have your daed's old room." Aunt Verna spoke up from across the room, where she sat in the rocking chair near the fireplace.

Elsie shook her head. "It's better for you and Uncle Lester to sleep downstairs. With his arthritis, climbing the steps would be too hard."

"Well, it's only for a few more days." Aunt Verna smiled. "I read in the paper that there's no snow in the forecast for several days, and I called one of our drivers. He's coming to get us Monday afternoon, so we'll soon be out of your hair."

"You don't have to be in a hurry to leave." John spoke loudly, no doubt compensating for Aunt Verna's hearing loss. "We've enjoyed being with you over the holidays and appreciate all you've done to help out."

"We were glad to be here, but it's time to head home." Aunt Verna glanced toward the kitchen, where her husband had gone to refill his coffee cup a few minutes ago. "Lester is eager to get back to the comforts of our own home." Her voice lowered. "He's not used to so much activity. I think the kinner get on his *naerfe* sometimes."

Elsie didn't respond because she didn't want to hurt her aunt's feelings, but living under the same roof with Aunt Verna and Uncle Lester this past week had gotten on her nerves a few times, too. In addition to practically yelling so her aunt could hear, Elsie had kept busy following behind Aunt Verna to close the refrigerator and cupboard doors. Her aunt was easily sidetracked, and a few times when she'd been cooking something on the stove, she'd wandered off to do something else and nearly burned whatever had been in the pot. Then there was the matter of Uncle Lester trying to do things he shouldn't and having to listen to Aunt Verna get after him.

"It's good to know Scott's home from the hospital now and is doing quite well," Elsie said, deciding they needed a change of subject.

Aunt Verna cupped one hand around her ear. "Did you say something about Scott and a bell?"

Elsie cleared her throat as she resisted the urge to roll her eyes. "No, I said, 'It's good to know Scott's home from the hospital now and is doing quite well.'"

"Jah. That boy gave us all quite

34

a scare."

Uncle Lester entered the living room empty-handed. "Where's the coffee you went after?" John asked.

"I sat at the kitchen table and drank it," he replied. "Wanted to read *The Budget* and see if any of the scribes from our home area had written anything interesting."

John quirked an eyebrow. "Did they?"

"Nope. At least nothin' I thought was interesting." Uncle Lester took a seat on the couch beside John. "It was mostly about the weather and who the visiting ministers were at their last church service."

The topic of church made Elsie realize that, as long as they lived in Dad's house, they'd go to every-other-week services in his district, rather than their own, since it was much closer. Once the weather improved, they would visit their own church district whenever possible.

"What did you say, Lester?" Aunt Verna called from across the room.

He flapped his hand. "Nothing, Verna. It's not worth mentioning."

"You must have thought whatever you said was worth mentioning, or you wouldn't have said it. I wish you'd speak a little louder and slower when you talk. Sometimes I can't keep up, because you talk too fast."

Uncle Lester glanced at Elsie and lifted his shoulders in a brief shrug. Then, speaking slow and loud, he repeated what he'd first said.

The knitting needles Aunt Verna held clicked noisily. "I always find it interesting to read about what other people are doing. Every little detail is fascinating to me."

"You would say that. Maybe you ought to see about becoming one of the scribes. Then you could write whatever you want."

Aunt Verna looked at Lester and wrinkled her nose. "I'm not a writer; I'm a reader."

Just then, Mary burst into the room. "Hope tripped and fell over something. Now she has a bloody nose."

Elsie groaned.

"It's okay. Stay where you are." John rose to his feet. "I'll take care of it."

Elsie leaned her head back and closed her eyes. She hoped things would go better in the coming year.

Akron, Ohio

"Happy New Year! It's so nice you could join us for dinner today," Kristi's mother said when their new youth pastor, Darin Underwood, entered the house.

He smiled and handed her a bottle of sparkling cider. "After last night's New Year's Eve party with the teens at church, it's nice to be someplace where it's a little quieter."

Mom motioned toward Kristi. "You remember my daughter, don't you?"

Darin nodded before stuffing his gray gloves into his coat pockets. "It's nice to see you again, Kristi."

"It's good to see you, too." Kristi blinked a few times and smiled. "Can I take your jacket?"

"Sure. Just give me a sec." He removed his jacket and gave it to Kristi.

After hanging it in the hall closet, she led the way to the living room, where Dad sat reading the newspaper.

"Glad you could make it." Dad rose from his seat and shook Darin's hand. "JoAnn and Kristi made pork and sauerkraut for dinner. Sure hope you like it."

"It's a recipe I got from an Amish cookbook I bought before Christmas," Kristi said.

Darin sniffed the air. "So that must be what I smell. It's hard to hide the tangy odor of sauerkraut."

"I hope you're not opposed to eating it." Dad gestured to the kitchen. "My wife should have asked ahead of time if your taste buds lean toward sauerkraut."

"I'm fine with it. Whenever I get a hot dog and sauerkraut's available, I always put some on." He wiggled his brows. "Think I could eat a good hot dog every day."

Kristi cringed. She preferred having variety in her diet. The idea of eating the same meal every day made her nauseous. If their new youth leader wasn't joking about being able to eat a hot dog every day, then his eating habits apparently didn't lean toward the healthy side of things. After Dad told Darin to take a seat, she excused herself to help Mom.

"Come here, Kristi," Mom whispered when she entered the kitchen. "Darin's cute, isn't he? Did you see how his blue eyes lit up when he first came in and saw you?"

Kristi lifted her chin toward the ceiling, gazing at a small strand of cobweb hanging over them that Mom must have missed the last time she cleaned. "He's probably glad to have been invited for a free meal. A healthier one than he normally eats, I might add." She lowered her voice. "I have a feeling

Darin lives on junk food."

"What are you basing that on?"

"He told Dad he likes hot dogs and could eat one every day."

"I'm sure he was only kidding." Mom tapped Kristi's shoulder. "You really should get to know the man before you judge his eating habits."

Wanting to change the topic, Kristi gestured to the stove. "Should I start dishing things up so we can eat?"

"That would be good. While you're doing that, I'll light the candles on the dining-room table." She smiled at Kristi. "Candlelight adds a little romance to any meal."

After her mother left the room, Kristi released a sigh. She hoped

Mom hadn't set this dinner up in an effort to play matchmaker. From the few times Kristi had spoken with Darin, he seemed nice enough. But she wasn't sure about beginning a new relationship with any man. Besides, she didn't know if Darin was even interested in her.

As they sat around the table a short time later, eating pork roast, sauerkraut, mashed potatoes, green beans, and fruit salad, Kristi found herself comparing Darin to Joel. It wasn't a fair thing to do, since her relationship with Joel was over, but she couldn't seem to help it. Darin's hair was blond, and his eyes were deep blue. Joel's brown eyes matched his dark wavy hair. But it wasn't their appearances she reflected on. It was the difference in their personalities. Darin was a jokester and had already told more corny jokes since they'd sat down to eat than Kristi had heard in the last year from other sources. While being "Mr. Funnyman" may go over well with the youth at their church, Kristi found it a bit annoying. Joel had a sense of humor, too, but he'd never spouted off one joke after another and then laughed at his own wisecracks the way Darin had been doing today. Mom certainly thought he was funny. She'd chuckled after and even during every one of his jokes. Was she only being polite, or did she really think he was that funny?

Kristi glanced over at Dad. He

seemed engrossed in eating and had left most of the chatting up to Mom and Darin during the meal. Kristi, too, had been rather quiet; but then, it was hard to get in a word with Darin monopolizing much of the conversation.

When they finished eating, Kristi excused herself to clear the table. Mom joined her in the kitchen a few minutes later. "Darin is sure humorous, isn't he?" Mom snickered. "The joke he told about the farmer who lost his chicken was so funny. I'm glad we invited him today. We all needed a good laugh."

Kristi silently opened the dishwasher and put the glasses inside.

Mom began rinsing the plates before handing them to Kristi. "I think Darin likes you, dear. Didn't you see the way he kept smiling in your direction?"

She shrugged.

"How do you feel about him?" Mom passed Kristi the bowl she'd rinsed.

"I don't know Darin well enough yet to say for sure, but so far I'm not feeling any chemistry between us."

"Give it some time. Once you get to know each other better, your feelings could change." Mom bumped Kristi's arm. "I wasn't immediately attracted to your father, either, but after we dated awhile, he sort of grew on me."

Kristi tapped her foot impatiently. "Darin and I are not dating, Mom."

"But you could be. Would you go out with him if he asked?"

"I don't know — maybe."

Mom's lips lifted at the corners as she rinsed some of the silverware. "I bet he will ask you soon."

"We'll see." Kristi continued loading the dishwasher. If Darin told more jokes while they ate dessert, she might look for an excuse to go home early.

Joel stared out the living-room window at the snow still on the ground. Even though most of the roads had been cleared, he'd only been driving his work truck to get around. As much as he wanted to take the Corvette out for a spin, he wouldn't chance crashing it during

47

the snowy season. Besides, if he took the car out on the roads, it would probably be filthy by the time he came home. Slush and mud seemed to be everywhere now that some of the snow had melted.

He looked up at the gray sky and wondered when the next snow-storm would arrive. From what he'd heard on a recent weather forecast, the next few days would be rain and clouds, but another snowstorm might follow.

Bored, Joel flopped onto the couch and turned on the TV. One of the channels was airing a show based on a romance novel. The male and female leads sat on a couch, kissing. The young woman had auburn hair, which reminded him of Kristi.

I wonder what she did to ring in the New Year. Has she found someone new and started dating again? He thought about last year and how much fun he'd had with Kristi as they celebrated the New Year. They'd talked about their hopes and dreams for the future and discussed wedding plans, even though they hadn't set a date.

Joel picked up his cell phone and scrolled down to her number, fighting the urge to call. *If I did, she'd probably ignore it, and I'd end up talking to her voice mail, like all the other times I've called since she broke up with me.* It didn't take a genius to know Kristi had made a clean break. However, a place in

Joel's heart hoped she would change her mind and give him another chance. *Once I've done a selfless act that's acceptable to my sisters and Aunt Verna, maybe Kristi will see me in a different light.*

He closed his eyes, picturing her pretty face. *If I could only see her again, even from a distance, it might give me a ray of hope.*

Forcing his contemplations to go in a different direction, Joel thought about the Christmas presents he'd bought for his sisters and their families. He had left them with Aunt Verna before he and Elsie had gone to the hospital to see about Scott but never heard a word about whether anyone liked what he'd gotten them. *So much for my sisters*

and aunt seeing the gifts as a selfless act. I'm gonna have to come up
with something better than that. My
bank account's shrinking, and I need
money soon.

CHAPTER 3

Charm

"The house seems quiet, doesn't it?" John asked as he and Elsie sat on the living-room sofa, eating popcorn and drinking hot cider Monday evening. The fire popped and danced behind the grate, giving off warm, welcoming heat and cozy light.

"*Jah.* During the holidays there's so much preparation and getting together with family and friends. Now we get to settle back and reflect on the moments, since most everything has calmed down." She took a sip from her mug. The cider was nice and tangy. For the first time since their house had caught fire, she felt herself relax a bit. It was good to sit with her husband and visit. The children were up- stairs in bed — even Blaine and Glen, who both had to get up early for work tomorrow morning. Aunt Verna and Uncle Lester returned to their own home early this after- noon, so Elsie had moved her and John's things to the downstairs master bedroom. Their sons said earlier it would be nice they didn't have to share a room anymore. It wasn't that the young men didn't get along; they both needed their own space.

Elsie remembered when she and Arlene once shared a bedroom in this house. It had been all right when they were young girls, but after they'd become teenagers, a few conflicts arose, despite their closeness. When John built the house he and Elsie lived in after they were married, he'd made sure there were plenty of bedrooms. It had been nice for each of their children to have their own room. Here, with only three bedrooms upstairs, Hope and Mary had to share a room. So far they didn't seem to mind, but if they lived here much longer, the girls might start fussing with each other, the way Elsie and Arlene used to do.

"You're awfully quiet." John touched Elsie's arm. "Are you feeling *mied* tonight, or is something wrong?"

"I'm reflecting on the past, and wondering how long our girls will get along if they have to keep sharing a bedroom."

"We'll rebuild as soon as we can." He refilled his bowl with more popcorn from the larger bowl on the coffee table. "If we had your inheritance, we could begin as soon as the weather improves."

Elsie looked down at her hands. "There's nothing I can do about it, John."

"Maybe your aunt would concede and let you open your envelopes now. We could all use the money

— even Joel."

Blinking rapidly, she turned to face him. "Do you think Dad would have put such a perplexing provision in his will if he didn't have a good reason for it?"

"I . . . I don't know, Elsie. Your daed wasn't like most people I know. He had some unusual habits and saw and did things a bit differently than most. I doubt he thought of the impact it will have on you, Arlene, and Doris if Joel doesn't come through."

"You're right, but Dad cared about his family and wanted the best for each of us. He must have believed Joel would eventually meet the requirements set forth in the will."

"I'm not sure he ever will." John laced his fingers together. "If your daed wanted the best for his daughters, then he would have allowed you to open your envelopes and acquire whatever he had in mind for you. By making you wait till Joel does an act of kindness . . ."

"A heartfelt, selfless act," she corrected.

"Jah, okay. Anyway, by making you wait till then, it's as though you, Arlene, and Doris are being punished for your *bruder's* selfishness." He crossed his arms. "If you want my opinion, only Joel should have to wait to open his envelope until he does the proper deed."

Elsie didn't admit it to John, but she'd thought the same thing numerous times since they'd discovered Dad's will in his freezer. Even so, it wouldn't be right to go against the stipulation he'd set forth so she could have her share of whatever Dad had left for her. She leaned her head on her husband's shoulder and closed her eyes. "It'll work out in God's time. We just need to be patient."

Farmerstown
Arlene pulled the pins from her bun and began brushing her long, silky hair. She glanced at the mirror hanging on the bedroom wall and noticed the dark circles under her eyes. After all the lost sleep she'd had during Scott's ordeal, she still didn't feel caught up on her

rest, so she'd decided to go to bed earlier than usual tonight. An inspirational novel lay on her nightstand that she'd started to read but put on hold. It would be nice to do some leisure reading before drifting off to sleep this evening.

The children were already in bed, and Larry had gone out to the barn a short time ago to check on one of their cats that had been in a fight the other day and ended up with an abscess on its head. Her husband had always given their animals good care. Not like the person Arlene had read about in the paper the other day, who'd lost two of his horses because he'd neglected them.

Such a shame, she thought, remembering how well her dad had taken care of the horses he'd raised. *Dad may have been a bit eccentric, but he never neglected his animals or children.*

She moved over to stand by the window. It was a clear, starry night, with no snow in sight. Arlene sighed, twisting her fingers around the ends of her hair. The old year had ended on a frightening note, but a new year was beginning, and she hoped things would improve.

Thankfully, Scott was feeling better; although he wouldn't be allowed to return to school for at least another week. Arlene wasn't taking any chances with her son's life. Too many germs could be passed around at school, and

Scott's immune system wasn't as strong as it should be yet.

In addition to her concern for his health, Arlene worried about the hospital bills that would soon be coming in. With only Larry working to provide for their needs, she wondered if she ought to seek employment. *Maybe I could get a job waitressing at one of the restaurants in Charm,* she thought. *I probably wouldn't make a lot, but at least it would be something to help out.*

"Didn't you say you were going to bed?" Larry asked, entering the room.

She turned from the window to face him. "I am."

"Then how come you're standing in front of the *fenschder?*"

"I was thinking."

He smiled, moving to stand beside her. "I hope they were good thoughts."

"Some were. Some not so good."

"Is it something we should talk about?"

Arlene nodded and lowered herself to the end of the bed. When Larry joined her there, she instinctively clasped his hand. "I'm grateful Scott's okay, but I'm worried about our finances."

"We've had money issues before and come through it." He pointed to the Bible lying on the table next to his side of the bed. "God has always provided for us."

"Jah, but maybe He expects us to do something, too."

"Like what?"

She released his hand, rocking back and forth with her arms folded. "What would you think of me getting a job? Maybe I could work at one of the nearby restaurants."

Shaking his head briskly, Larry pressed his thumb to his chest. "No way! I'm the bread winner in this family. Your place is here, taking care of the kinner as well as the house."

"But they're all in school most of the day. And if they came home after school let out and I wasn't home from work yet, I'm sure they could fend for themselves a short time."

"No." He rose from the bed and

looked directly into her eyes. "It's better for them and you if you're not working outside the house." As if the matter were settled, Larry opened the closet door and took out his pajamas. Then he came to where she still sat, bent down, and kissed her forehead. "Try not to worry. Somehow, some way, the money to pay the hospital bills will be there when we need it."

Arlene wished she could be that certain. If she could open the envelope Dad had left her, their financial problems would most likely be solved.

Akron

Exhausted from a hard day at work on a job that wouldn't pay much,

Joel crashed on the couch as soon as he'd eaten supper. He tried watching TV for a bit, but his eyes grew heavy, and soon he dozed off.

Sometime later, he was roused from a deep sleep by the rumble of a car. Feeling as though he was in a stupor, he rolled off the couch and stood. "Now who in the world could that be?"

Joel stumbled over to the window, pulled the curtain aside, and peered out. One of his outside lights was burned out, making it hard to tell what the vehicle looked like. Joel thought it might be a truck, but he couldn't be sure. He figured if it was someone he knew, they would turn off the ignition and come up to the house. Instead, the driver of the rig sat in the driveway a few minutes, then drove up to the garage, backed up, and headed for Joel's shop.

Oh, no! Warning bells went off in Joel's head. He quickly grabbed the brightest flashlight he owned and jerked the door open. Stepping onto the porch, Joel saw his own breath as he shined the light on the vehicle. Sure enough, it was a truck, but he didn't recognize it.

Who is that? He moved over to the steps to get a better look. Suddenly, the door on the driver's side of the vehicle opened. A tall man with a scruffy beard stepped out.

"What do you want?" Joel called, holding the flashlight so he could see what the man was doing.

The bearded fellow didn't look in Joel's direction as he reached into the back of his truck, took out a cardboard box, and started walking unsteadily toward the shop. He was clearly drunk or maybe high on something.

"Stop where you are!" Joel hollered. "Get back in your truck or I'm calling the sheriff!"

The man hesitated, then started moving again in a zigzag pattern.

Joel's heart pounded as he squeezed tighter on the flashlight. His fingers were numb from the cold, but his body felt like it was overheating. *If I had a gun, I'd fire it over that guy's head. Maybe he'd be scared enough to hightail it outa here.* Joel shouted at the fellow once more, this time with a little more force. *I sure hope he doesn't have a gun. If he does, I could be in trouble.*

Even though Joel was concerned for his own welfare, he was more worried about his prized Corvette in the shop. "This is your last warning," he yelled at the top of his lungs. "The sheriff lives nearby. It won't take him long to get here."

The bearded man stopped walking and turned to face Joel. Then he wobbled back to his truck, placed the box he held inside, and got in. He sat behind the wheel several seconds, then turned the vehicle around, drove up the driveway, and headed out onto the main road.

Joel stood watching to be sure the man wasn't coming back, then he ducked back inside and grabbed his cell phone. "As if I don't have enough to worry about," he muttered, before dialing 911. Joel gave the best description he could of the man and his vehicle. The lady on the phone, who worked for dispatch, told Joel she'd send a patrol car out to his address and they'd search the area to see if they could spot the trespasser's truck. If the vehicle returned, Joel was to call back right away.

He clicked off the phone and slid it into his pocket. When he brought his hands up to his face, he noticed they were shaking. Having an uninvited visitor on his property had unnerved him. *If I had a watchdog, it might have dissuaded the intruder — not to mention, given me a warning that someone was there.*

After pondering the idea further, Joel decided he would go to the local animal shelter in the morning to see about getting a dog. He also needed to fix the outside light that had burned out.

"Maybe I should get an alarm system, too — at least for the shop," he mumbled. With a car that expensive on his property, Joel couldn't afford to take any chances. He should have taken care of this when he'd first bought the Vette.

Joel peered out the living-room window to be sure the strange man hadn't come back. He felt some relief knowing the sheriff would drive by his place and check around the area. There was no way he could get much sleep tonight. In fact, he probably wouldn't sleep well until he'd made sure his property was well protected.

CHAPTER 4

The next day before going to work, Joel replaced the yard light that had been out, then drove to the animal shelter to look for a dog. Before he left, the sheriff's office called to let him know the guy who'd come on his property had tried the same thing at a house a mile down the road. He'd been caught and taken to jail, so that was a relief. Even so, Joel needed to make sure his property was protected from intruders. He wanted a dog big enough to be intimidating but not so large it would cost Joel a lot of money to feed. A good strong bark was also a must.

He wandered up and down the aisles, peering into each of the dogs' cages. There weren't many to choose from. Joel figured they were probably picked over because people came here looking for dogs to give as Christmas gifts. One dog in particular caught Joel's attention — not for himself, because the critter was too small. The brown-and-white terrier mix reminded him of the one Doris had as a child. She'd named it Bristleface and taught the yappy critter all kinds of tricks. Joel would never forget how hard his sister cried when Bristleface ran into the road and got hit by a car. The dog had been killed on impact. After that, Doris had never asked for another dog.

"She might like one now, though," Joel said aloud. It wouldn't replace the baby she'd lost, but it would be good company. Since the dog looked so much like the one she'd had before, Doris might be happy to have it. *It could even be the selfless act I'm supposed to do.* He smiled to himself. *Once Doris sees the mutt, I bet she'll put in a good word for me with Aunt Verna.*

He crouched down and stuck his fingers through the cage, letting the dog lick them. "What do you say, Bristleface Two? Would ya like a new home?"

Yip! Yip! The dog's tail wagged as it wiggled around. It was the answer Joel needed. Setting aside his idea of getting a watchdog for himself, Joel hurried to the front of the shelter to let the person in charge know he'd found the right dog for his sister. Maybe an alarm system for his shop and better lighting would be all he would need at this time.

Joel climbed into his truck with the dog and scratched the side of his head. *Now what?* His original intent was to find a dog for himself, take it to his place, then head to the job he'd started yesterday. Now he had the yappy terrier to deal with, and he didn't have time to go all the way to Doris's house this morning. He could take the critter to his place and lock it in the house while he was at work, but the dog might not be housebroken, so that wasn't a good choice.

"Guess I'll have to be late for work whether I like it or not," he muttered, moving the dog off his lap and onto the passenger's seat. Sometimes Joel didn't think things through well enough; this was one of those times. *I should have waited till I finished working for the day to visit the animal shelter. Sure hope Doris is home when I get there, or I'll really be in a fix.*

He picked up his cell phone and called the owner of the house where he had been working, to let them know he'd be a few hours late. When that was done, he started up the truck and headed for the freeway, going south. The first few miles, the dog rode calmly, until it started throwing up.

"Are you kidding me?" Joel looked over at the poor mutt, while he brought his vehicle to a stop on the shoulder of the road. Then he grabbed a rag from under his seat to wipe up the stinky stuff. He opened his window, hoping to get rid of the putrid odor, but the icy-cold air blowing in wasn't pleasant. The trip to Doris's would be miserable.

Berlin

Because Brian was working, Doris had hired a driver to take her to an afternoon appointment to get her leg x-rayed. If it had healed as well as the doctor hoped, she'd get the cast off next week. After the appointment, she planned to meet her friend Anna for an early supper.

Doris was able to get around better now, with the aid of one crutch or a cane, so her sisters didn't come over as often as they had before to help out. When Elsie and her family moved into Dad's house, Doris had been worried Aunt Verna and Uncle Lester might come back here to her place to stay. She loved her aunt and uncle, but she was glad when they'd returned to their home in Burton. A few days of shouting in order to be heard by Aunt Verna was tolerable, but any longer became unbearable. Usually the shouting wouldn't bother her so much, but Doris was sensitive about everything these days. She was still trying to come to grips with having lost her baby, and seeing her sisters go through trials of their own on Christmas Eve had only worsened her depression.

What I need is to go back to work at the restaurant, where I'll be busy and around people, she thought. After her cast came off, she'd be faced with physical therapy, so it could be several weeks or even months before she was able to be on her feet long enough to complete a shift at Der Dutchman.

Hearing a car come up the driveway, Doris went to the living-room window and looked out. At first, she thought her driver had mixed up the time and arrived early. She did a double-take when she saw Joel's truck pull up in front of the house and jerked her head when he got out of his vehicle with a scruffy-looking dog in his arms.

What is Joel doing here, and why does he have that hund *with him?* Doris hobbled to the door and opened it.

"Hey, look what I've got for you!" He was all smiles as he held the dog close to Doris's face.

She leaned her head back when it tried to lick her nose. "You bought this dog for me?" Doris couldn't imagine what would possess her brother to do such a thing. She'd never mentioned wanting a dog — to Joel or anyone else, for that matter.

Still grinning, he nodded. "I got it at the animal shelter in Akron this morning. It looks so much like the dog you had when we were kids, I couldn't resist buying it for you." Joel stroked the terrier's pointy little ears. "Thought maybe you could call it Bristleface Two."

Doris leaned against the doorframe for support and warmth. "It was nice of you to think of me, Joel, but I can't take care of a dog."

"Oh, you mean, because of your leg?" He gestured to her cast.

"It's not that. I'll be going back to work as soon as I'm able, and no one will be here to keep an eye on the dog." She sucked in her bottom lip. "Besides, I lost my desire to have a hund after Bristleface died."

Joel pressed one hand to his temple. "So you won't take the mutt?"

"No, sorry, I can't." She stepped back into the house.

"So what am I supposed to do with him?"

Doris shrugged. "You could keep him or see if someone else in the family would like a dog."

He moved his hand to the back of his neck. "I don't have time to run all over the place, trying to find a home for the critter. I have a job to do and need to head there now."

"Well, you can't leave him here. My driver will be coming this afternoon to take me to an appointment, and I'm meeting Anna for supper after that."

Joel glanced at the dog and frowned. "It's out of the way, but maybe I'll stop by Arlene's place and see if one of her kids would like the mutt."

"That's a good idea." Her body lacked tension and stress as she patted the dog's head. Doris had felt this way when she owned her own little terrier when she was a girl. The dog made her forget all the problems she'd had at school or with her siblings — at least for a little while. This dog might do the same, but she didn't want the extra responsibility.

Wait a minute, she thought. *I know who Joel should give the hund to.* "You know, Scott's still out of school, recuperating from his surgery. I'll bet he'd like a dog to play with."

"You could be right, Sis. Don't know why I didn't think of it." Joel turned to go. "Have a nice day. Oh, and tell Anna I said hello."

Doris stood in the doorway, watching him get in his truck and drive away. As the wind picked up, she quickly shut the door. Even though the sun shone brightly, the air was bitter cold. She should have put a jacket or her shawl on before answering the door.

Farmerstown

Arlene stepped onto the porch and was about to shake some throw rugs when Joel's truck pulled into the yard. Scott must have seen it, too, for he poked his head out the door. "Look, Mom, Uncle Joel's here. Bet he came to see how I'm doin'."

Arlene hoped it was true, but her brother had only shown up once to see Scott since his surgery, using the excuse that he'd been busy with work. *No one should ever be too busy for family,* she thought.

"Go back inside, Son. It's icy cold out here. You can visit with your uncle when he comes inside." She remained in place, holding the rugs.

Scott's lower lip protruded, but he did as she asked. Watching Joel get out of his truck, Arlene was surprised to see that he was holding a dog.

Joel smiled when he stepped onto the porch. "How's Scott doing?"

"Better, but not quite ready to return to school."

"I'm glad he's doin' better. The kid's probably happy he gets to stay home awhile."

"He is, but he still has to do his schoolwork. Scott's brother has been bringing it home for him." She stared at the dog in Joel's arms. The critter had a shiny black nose, reminding her of a wet olive. "Aren't you going to introduce me to your new friend, Joel?"

"Oh, well . . . I actually thought maybe Scott might like to have this little fellow." Joel patted the terrier's head. "That is, if it's all right with you."

Arlene bit the inside of her cheek, wondering if this was her brother's attempt at doing another so-called selfless act. Giving the dog to her son might make Joel believe he had an easy chance at getting his portion of the will, but she wouldn't vote for it and didn't think her sisters or Aunt Verna would, either. On the other hand, Scott had been bored since he'd come home from the hospital, so having a dog to fuss over could be a good thing.

"Come inside, and we'll see what

Scott thinks." She draped the rugs over the porch railing and opened the door.

As soon as they entered the house, Scott greeted them, smiling from ear to ear. "What have ya got, Uncle Joel? Is that your cute little hund?"

"It's yours if you want it." Joel handed the dog to Scott.

"Wow, ya mean it? I get to keep him for my very own?"

"Yep. Every boy needs a good dog."

Scott held the terrier close and snickered when it licked his chin. "I think he likes me. What's his name?"

"That's up to you." Joel stroked the dog's head. "He reminds me of a dog your aunt Doris had when she was a girl, so if you can't come up with something better, you could call him Bristleface Two."

"Can I just name him 'Bristleface,' without the word 'two'?"

"Don't see why not." Joel looked at Arlene. "Sorry I can't stay, but I'm already late for work. I'll come by some other time to see how Scott and his new dog are doing." He paused and gave Scott's shoulder a pat. "Take care of Bristleface, ya hear?"

Scott's grin never left his face. "I will. You can be sure of it."

As Arlene watched Joel get in his truck and drive off, she couldn't help thinking her brother's heart had softened a bit.

Berlin

As soon as Doris entered Boyd & Wurthmann Restaurant, she spotted Anna sitting at a table near the window. She headed that way and took a seat across from her.

"How'd your doctor's appointment go?" Anna asked.

"I didn't see the doctor today. Just had an X-ray of my leg taken. I'll see the doctor in a few days to get the results. Then he'll decide how soon the cast can come off."

"I bet you're anxious for that."

"Jah." Doris glanced down at her cast. "I'm tired of the cumbersome thing and will be glad when I'm able to go back to waitressing."

"Have you thought about looking for something closer to home?" Anna tilted her body toward Doris. "Maybe they're hiring here."

Doris removed her shawl and placed it across her lap. "This would be a nice place to work, I suppose, but Der Dutchman is a bigger restaurant. More people seem to go there, which means more tips."

"I see what you mean." Anna gestured to her menu. "I already know what I want, but feel free to take your time deciding. Since school's out for the day, I don't have to rush."

"Me neither. Brian will be working late this evening, and I told my driver I'd call for a ride home after I had supper with you." Doris studied the menu, although she didn't know why. She planned to have her favorite turkey club sandwich, with a cup of chicken noodle soup.

When their waitress came, they told her what they wanted. Anna ordered a cold plate, of cottage cheese, Jell-O, fruit, trail bologna, and swiss cheese. She also asked for a bowl of chili.

"How are things at school?" Doris asked, after taking a sip of water. "Have things settled down now that Christmas is over?"

"Jah. Everything's pretty much back to normal. But with Valentine's Day coming next month, the scholars will soon begin making cards to give each other. Of course when I bring heart-shaped cookies and fruit punch for a treat on Valentine's Day, they'll get pretty excited."

Doris smiled, remembering how much she'd enjoyed making Valentine cards for her classmates, as well as family members and friends from their church district. Even many of the boys, including Joel, seemed to like exchanging Valentine's Day greetings.

Thinking about her brother, Doris remembered to tell Anna that she'd seen Joel earlier today and he'd said to say hello.

"That was nice of him." Anna cupped her chin in her hands. "I think I'm finally ready to let go of my feelings for Joel."

Doris blinked a couple of times. "Really? How did that happen?"

Anna's cheeks reddened. "Well, I've met someone."

"Is it someone I know?" Doris leaned in closer.

"I don't think so. He's new to our area. His name is Melvin Mast. I met him a few weeks ago when he came to the school Christmas program with his folks."

"I'm confused." Doris glanced down, realizing she was fumbling with her napkin, so she unfolded it and placed it on her lap. "If he's new to the area, why was he at the program?"

"His younger cousin attends my school."

"Have you seen Melvin since then?"

Anna nodded. "He's in our church district, so I've seen him at church a few times. He also dropped by the school the other day to pick up his cousin, and . . ." She paused to drink some water. "He asked if I'd like to go out to supper with him sometime."

Doris laughed. "My goodness, this new fellow didn't waste any time, did he?"

"Well, we're both in our late twenties and not getting any younger." Anna fiddled with her spoon. "I don't know yet if Melvin's the one, but I do think he's good-looking, and he seems very kind."

Doris reached across the table

and touched her friend's hand. "I wish you all the best."

She felt relieved that Anna would no longer be pining for Joel. She'd done it far too long.

CHAPTER 5

North Canton, Ohio

Kristi shivered against the cold as she entered the North Canton Skate Center with Darin and fifteen eager teens from their church youth group. It was the first Saturday of February, and after Darin had practically begged her to accompany him, she'd agreed to act as a chaperone. While Kristi wasn't by any means a professional on roller skates, it was good exercise and a chance to do something fun for a change. Last week she'd worked several back-to-back shifts at the nursing home and needed a little downtime.

As the teens chatted with each other and their new youth leader, Kristi sat on a bench by herself to put on her skates. She hadn't gone roller skating since she was a teenager and had forgotten how noisy it could be. Between the hum of voices, and the music blaring overhead, it was hard to think.

"Let's get something to eat before we start skating." Irv, a fifteen-year-old freckle-faced boy, pointed to the snack bar. "I need a few hot dogs to get me revved up."

Darin bobbed his head. "I'm with you on that. Anyone else want to eat now?"

Several hands went up, and then he turned to Kristi. "How about you? Should I order us both a hot dog with fries?"

"No thanks. Think I'll skate awhile, then see later on if they have anything healthier than hot dogs in the snack area."

Darin finished lacing up his skates and pushed a chunk of hair out of his face. "Okay, whatever you want to do is fine with me." He stood, did a few wobbly turns on his skates, and rolled off in the direction of the snack bar. Several of the teens followed, but a few went out on the rink.

Kristi watched the kids start skating. They seemed to get it right, without a problem. They made it look simple, in fact. Hopefully, it would be easy to skate out there, with the amount of bodies already filling up the ever-shrinking skating space.

There are a lot of people here tonight, she mused. *We'll be packed in tightly, like a tin of sardines wearing roller skates.*

A bit unsteady at first, Kristi inched her way along, until she, too, was on the rink. She would take it slow and easy until she felt more confident, because the last thing she needed was to fall and make a fool of herself.

She'd only been skating fifteen minutes when Darin, flailing his arms overhead, skated up to her with a big grin. "I'd forgotten how much fun skating could be. Haven't been at a rink in several years."

"Me neither. It took a while to get my balance." She smiled as he nodded and did a few awkward-looking turns.

"You weren't in the snack bar very long. Did you get anything to eat?"

"Sure did." He grinned and smacked his lips. "The hot dog was so good I practically inhaled it."

Kristi resisted the urge to give Darin her thoughts on the importance of a healthy diet. Instead, she gave a small wave and sailed right past him.

Half an hour later, she headed for the snack bar. The line was short, but she stood off to the side to figure out what to order. Her eyebrows drew in as she browsed the menu board. Kristi didn't care to eat most of the foods listed, since she preferred organic food with less sugar. Finally, she settled on a slice of pizza and a bottle of water. As she sat at one of the tables with her food, watching the skaters on the floor, she spotted a man who reminded her of Joel. He had the same thick, dark hair and short-cropped beard. However, this guy was skating with two small children, each holding his hand. He was obviously not Joel.

I shouldn't be thinking of Joel right now, Kristi berated herself. *What we once had is over, and it's time to move on.* How many times had she thought about him and given herself a mental shake? She picked up her slice of pizza and took a small bite. *If only things could have worked out differently between us.*

As Kristi got up from her seat to throw away her paper plate and napkin, she thought about Joel's family and wondered how they were all doing. She'd meant to go back to Der Dutchman Restaurant to see Doris again but hadn't made it. She'd been busy during the holidays, and now with the unpredictable weather, she didn't feel like driving down to Holmes County on roads that were often icy or covered in snow. Besides, it was hard to see Doris and not think about Joel.

"You coming back out to skate?" Darin skated up to her. "They just announced the next song is for couples only. Would you like to be my partner?"

Couples only? She nearly jumped. Her face, neck, and ears were impossibly hot. *Oh, my. Maybe Darin is interested in me.* Kristi hesitated but finally nodded. "Sure." She tossed the trash from her meal in the garbage, cleaned her hands with a disposable wipe, and followed him out to the skating floor.

Darin took her hand, and they skated easily along. *This is actually kind of fun.* Even though she doubted Darin would be a potential guy for her to go out with, she began to have second thoughts as she continued to skate with him. He seemed so gentle and kind. And the way his eyes sparkled when he talked to her made it feel almost like they were on a date. That thought was quickly dispelled, however, when two of the teens — Rick and Connie, skated up to them.

Connie's cheeks flushed pink, while her blue eyes danced merrily. "This is fun, isn't it, Darin?"

"Sure is." He grinned at Kristi. "We should do this again sometime."

Kristi couldn't believe Darin allowed the teens to call him by his first name. It seemed disrespectful. At the very least, Connie could have called him "Pastor Darin."

He acts like he's one of them, instead of their pastor, she thought when Darin let go of her hand and skated in circles around Rick and Connie. *He's just a big kid at heart.* Kristi guessed that wasn't all bad. Some people took life too seriously.

"Wanna see me skate backward?" Darin asked, returning to her side.

"Sure, if you want to." She looked at him and giggled nervously. *I hope neither of us falls.*

He turned and got in front of her, then reached out his hands. She was about to take hold of them when the guy who looked like he could be related to Joel came by, holding hands with the little girl Kristi had seen him with earlier. Being this close to the man, she realized he didn't resemble Joel as much as she'd first thought. His eyes were blue, not brown, and there was a slight hump in the middle of his nose. *Guess everyone has someone who resembles them,* she thought, clasping Darin's hands.

They skated for a while, facing each other, until Darin started skating too fast. Suddenly, he stumbled, let go of her hand, and fell.

"Are you okay?" Kristi stopped skating and reached out her hand to help him up.

"I don't think anything's broken, but my knees sure hurt." He gave her a sheepish grin. "Guess that's what I get for showin' off."

Holding tightly to Darin's hand, Kristi guided him off the floor and over to a bench. "Should I go to the snack bar and get some ice for your knees?"

"Yeah, I'd appreciate it."

Being careful not to fall herself, she made her way to the snack bar. When she returned with two small bags of ice, she found Darin surrounded by several of the girls from their church, all wearing concerned expressions.

"Thanks, Kristi." He took the ice from her and placed it on his injured knees. "It hurts more now that I'm sitting than it did when I fell."

Kristi checked his knees to be sure nothing was broken. "I think they're both just badly bruised, but the ice should help."

"It's kinda handy to have a nurse along to take care of me. Maybe we can go out for supper sometime next week, and I'll reward you for your kindness."

Kristi's face heated, and she turned her head away from him, hoping he wouldn't notice. "There's no need for that."

"Are you saying you don't want to go out for a meal?"

"No, of course not. I only meant —"

"Hey, Darin, my dad just called. He wants to know what time to pick me up at the church." Rick squatted in front of Darin, holding a cell phone. "What happened to you?"

Darin explained his accident, then told Rick to tell his dad he could pick him up in an hour. He looked up at Kristi. "Would you mind driving the van? I'm not going to do any more skating, and with my knees hurting, the idea of pressing either of my feet on the gas pedal or brake holds no appeal right now."

"I don't mind driving," she replied, relieved that he hadn't mentioned going out to dinner again. It could be construed as a date, and she wasn't ready for that.

Akron

When Kristi entered the church sanctuary the following morning, she spotted Darin sitting halfway down at one end of a pew. Several people stood in the aisle talking to him, so Kristi held back until they moved on.

"How are your knees?" she asked.

"Still a little tender this morning, and there's some swelling, but you were right — they are both bruised." He placed his hand on each knee and grimaced. "Ice helps some, but I wish there was something else I could put on the bruises."

"Actually, there is." Kristi reached into her purse and pulled out a tube of Arnica. "This is a homeopathic remedy available at most health food stores. Why don't you take it home and try it?" She handed the tube of medicine to him.

"Thanks, Kristi. I'll buy you a replacement as soon as I can."

"There's no need for that. I have another one at home." She removed her coat, draping it over one arm.

Darin slid over a ways. "Why don't you sit beside me? The service is about to start."

Kristi glanced at her parents, sitting in the row behind them, and couldn't help but notice Mom's giddy demeanor. *She was happy when I told her I'd gone skating with Darin and the teens last night, so she'd probably be thrilled if I sit with him now.*

The worship team had already started the first song, but other people were filing in, so Kristi could still take a seat with her parents. But she decided to sit beside Darin, so she slid in next to him.

Kristi set her purse on the floor by her feet and laid her coat over the back of the pew. She opened the bulletin and quickly scanned it to see what was on this week's agenda. Then she glanced around, feeling a little nervous. *Sure hope this doesn't start any rumors going around the church. The last thing I need is for people to think I'm making a play for our new youth pastor.*

Joel hadn't slept well — mostly because he'd had a dream about Kristi. She was still on his mind after he'd gotten dressed and eaten breakfast, and it bothered him a lot. *Why am I thinking about her all of a sudden? I haven't talked to Kristi for several months. Could the dream I had be a sign that I should contact her again?*

He squinted at his reflection in the hall mirror and released an impatient huff. *I wonder how she'd respond if I showed up at church today and tried talking to her. Would she listen? Would she consider giving me a second chance?*

Joel stepped into his bedroom, opened the closet door, and pulled out his nicest jacket. *If I hurry, I can probably make it to church before the service ends. Think I'll throw caution to the wind and give it a try.*

When Joel arrived at the church, his stomach quivered, and he began to have second thoughts. If Kristi was here today, she'd no doubt be sitting with her folks. Since neither of them cared that much for Joel, they might ask him to leave. For that matter, Kristi could just as easily tell him to get lost. But maybe with so many Christians around her, she'd be less apt to make an undesirable scene. *This could give me an edge,* he thought.

All those weeks after their breakup, Joel had tried to contact Kristi, and she'd never returned any of his calls. How much clearer could she make it?

He stepped into the entryway and hesitated. *It'd probably be best if I turn around now and head for home, but since I'm here, I may as well go through with it.*

Joel opened the door to the sanctuary and stepped inside, careful to shut it quietly. The worship team was on the platform, and some woman Joel had never met was reading scripture from the front of the room.

He stood there a few minutes, scanning the pews, hoping Kristi would be somewhere near the back. About halfway down, he spotted her, sitting beside a man with blond hair. He wasn't her dad.

Joel's heart started to pound, and his nerves wavered. Kristi's folks sat in the pew behind them, and the blond-headed guy was leaning close to Kristi, as though he was whispering something in her ear.

I'm too late. Joel's jaw clenched so hard his teeth clicked together. *She's already found someone else.* He felt heat behind his eyes, and his shoulders slumped in defeat. *Kristi.* Clutching his arm toward his chest, Joel turned and hurried out the door. This would be the last time he'd ever set foot in this church. It would also be the final time he'd try to make contact with her. He definitely needed to move on.

CHAPTER 6

Farmerstown

"It was nice having you and your family visit our church today," Arlene said as she and Elsie sat in the kitchen together, drinking tea. "And I'm glad you came here afterward so we'd have more time to chat." She reached down and patted Bristleface's head. He leaned against her chair, seeming to absorb the sweet attention.

"It's always good to visit with family." Elsie smiled, although there was no sparkle in her eyes. "I see Scott's new pet has taken a liking to you."

"Jah, this little terrier knows when he's got it made." Arlene wondered if her sister was trying to put on a brave front by talking about things other than what was actually on her mind. Elsie hadn't been the same since their house burned down. Arlene certainly understood how hard it could be to remain cheerful when tragedies occurred. Adding more tea to her near-empty cup, she said, "I wish Doris and Brian could have joined us, too."

"It would have been nice, but since Brian is down with the flu, I'm sure Doris didn't even go to their own church service today."

"It's understandable. She needs to take care of him. I hope for her sake she doesn't get sick, too." Arlene tapped the side of her mug.

Elsie added half a spoonful of sugar to her tea and stirred it around. "I'm glad her leg has finally healed and she's able to work at the restaurant again. I think she missed it, and with hospital and doctor bills to pay, they need the extra money coming in."

"How well I know." Arlene sighed. "I think we'll be paying on Scott's hospital bill till the end of this year."

"We all need money right now." Elsie bit her bottom lip. "I don't mean to sound greedy, but it would sure be nice if we could all open our envelopes to see how much Dad left us." She looked out the window, watching the birds eating from one of the feeders.

Arlene cleared her throat. "I'm sure he gave us equal shares of whatever his assets are, but if Joel doesn't do something we can all agree is a heartfelt, selfless act, we may never get whatever Dad wanted us to have."

Elsie drank some tea, then added a bit more sugar. "Have you heard anything from Joel lately?" she asked, looking back at her sister.

"No. Have you?"

"Huh-uh. Not since he came by a few weeks ago to see if we all liked our Christmas presents. I think he was hoping we'd say his gift-giving was a selfless act." Elsie pushed her chair back a ways to cross her legs.

Arlene folded her arms. "Same thing for when he gave Scott the dog. I heard from Aunt Verna a few weeks after that, and she said Joel had called and told her what he'd done."

"What'd she say in response?"

"Not a lot. Just said she told Joel she thought Scott would enjoy having the dog, but it wasn't a selfless act."

"Maybe our bruder isn't capable of doing something completely selfless. Whatever he's done so far has been with an ulterior motive." Elsie blew out a breath, rattling her lips. "He's trying too hard, and it's not heartfelt."

"What's not heartfelt?" Scott asked when he entered the room and squatted beside his dog.

"Nothing, Son." Arlene pointed at the terrier, still lying beside her feet. "I don't really like having your dog in the kitchen, but he has a persuasive way about him."

"I showed Uncle John and my cousins the tricks I've taught my hund, and I want Aunt Elsie to see what he can do."

Elsie rose from her chair. "I'll go out to the living room, and you can show me in there."

Scott's face lit up. "Okay! After that, I'm gonna play a song I learned on the harmonica Uncle Joel gave me." He looked up at Arlene. "Are ya comin', Mom?"

She nodded. "I'll be there as soon as I put our tea cups in the sink."

Scott headed for the living room with the dog at his heels, and Elsie followed.

Arlene smiled as she cleared the dishes from the table and placed them in the sink. Joel had done a good thing by giving Scott the mutt, but it really wasn't enough. He needed to do something sacrificial without trying to get anything in return. Unless her brother had a complete change of heart, it wasn't likely he'd ever do a good deed for anyone without expecting something back.

Elsie had felt uptight most of the day, but after laughing at Bristleface's antics as he did several tricks, she relaxed a bit. Laughter was good medicine. She remembered her mother had often quoted Proverbs 17:22: "A merry heart doeth good like a medicine: but a broken spirit drieth the bones." Her bones had certainly felt dry since they'd lost their house. She'd struggled to find any joy at all, but she still tried to hide her frustrations and despondency from the children. If they knew how disheartened their mother felt, it would upset them. Even John didn't know the extent of her depression. She'd shared a few of her thoughts with him, but most things she kept hidden in her heart. There was nothing her husband could do about their situation, so what was the point in saying anything? Truth was, John probably held in his thoughts and feelings, too. Some days Elsie wondered if anything in their lives would ever feel right again.

Thunder sounded in the distance, causing Elsie to rise from her seat in the rocking chair. She went to the living-room window and looked out. "It's snowing — really hard!"

Arlene and both of the men joined her at the window.

"You don't hear *dunner* when it's snowing very often," Larry commented. "I have a feeling we might be in for another storm."

"Could turn into a blizzard." John's brows furrowed. "I can hear the horses out in the barn, whinnying something awful."

Arlene slipped her arm around Elsie's waist. "I think it would be safer if you spent the night here."

Larry nodded. "I agree with my *fraa.* Sure wouldn't advise going home with a spooky horse in this kind of weather, even though Charm's not that far from here."

Elsie looked at John to get his reaction.

"I believe you're right, Larry," he replied. "If you're sure you don't mind, we'll crash here tonight. If things look better in the morning, we'll head back to Charm."

"What about *schul?*" Hope spoke up. "If we spend the night here, how am I gonna get to school on time tomorrow?"

"I'll take you there with my horse and buggy." John gave her shoulder a squeeze. "Try not to worry about it, okay? If the storm is too bad, school will probably be cancelled tomorrow, anyway."

Elsie shivered as another clap of thunder sounded. This one seemed a little closer than the last. The snow was falling harder. She was pretty sure they were in for a blizzard.

Hearing the thunder made her think about Dad and how lightning and thunder had struck the night he'd been killed in his tree house. She closed her eyes. *I miss you, Dad. I'd rather we had you here with us right now than be waiting to see how much of your money we were going to get.*

Joel had developed a headache soon after he'd left the church, but even though he'd taken something for it, the pounding pain remained.

It's probably from the stress of knowing I've lost Kristi for good, he told himself as he lay down on his bed. Joel had spent most of the day in bed, hoping some rest would help the headache go away, and he'd only gotten up once to get a bite to eat.

A clap of thunder brought his head off the pillow. "Dunner this time of the year?" Joel didn't know why, but the German-Dutch word rolled off his tongue. He got up and

129

looked out the window. It was snowing hard, and the wind blew furiously. Another boom sounded, and a vision of his dad came to mind. *What must it have been like for him, up in the tree house when the lightning struck?* He shuddered at the thought.

For the first time since his father's death, Joel teared up. A knot formed in his stomach, and a gut-wrenching sob tore from his throat. "Oh, Dad, I have so many regrets." It grieved him to know he hadn't had a chance to say goodbye or make amends with Dad before he died. But it was too late to do anything about it now.

Blurry-eyed, Joel's gaze came to rest on the black book with golden embossed letters along the spine lying on his dresser. It was the NIV Bible Kristi had given him last year at Christmas. He'd taken it to church with him a few times, hoping to impress her, but had never opened it when he was at home. But now Joel felt a strong need to open it.

He picked up the Bible and sat on the end of his bed. A green ribbon stuck out, so he opened it to that section. After reading several verses, Joel paused at 1 John 3:17: "If anyone has material possessions and sees a brother or sister in need but has no pity on them, how can the love of God be in that person?"

He continued to read verses 18, 19, and 20: "Dear children, let us not love with words or speech but with actions and in truth. This is how we know that we belong to the truth and how we set our hearts at rest in his presence: If our hearts condemn us, we know that God is greater than our hearts, and he knows everything."

Tears stinging his eyes, Joel read on, until he came to verse 23: "And this is his command: to believe in the name of his Son, Jesus Christ, and to love one another as he commanded us."

As the words from the passage pierced his heart, Joel fell to his knees beside his bed. The truth of his transgressions hit him with the force of a strong wind. His self-centeredness and deceitfulness had caused him to lose Kristi, and they had put a wedge between him and his family for years. He hadn't been a good son and had brought shame to his father. *No wonder Dad was so hard on me. He wanted me to see the error of my ways and become the man I should be.*

"Father in heaven," Joel prayed tearfully, "I've been so selfish, always thinking of myself instead of others. I believe in the name of Jesus and ask Your forgiveness. Let Your love flow into my heart, and help me to be a better person. I commit my life to You."

When his prayer was finished, Joel stood, holding the Bible against his chest. The seed that had been planted when he'd attended the

Amish church with his parents and siblings as a child had finally taken root.

A deep ache pressed against Joel's heart. He felt the pain of what his sisters had recently gone through as though it were his own. Joel sank to his bed as a realization hit him. He knew what he had to do. The only problem was, it might take some time to make it happen.

CHAPTER 7

Berlin

It was the third Saturday of March, and Doris had been back to work for over a month. While she found her job enjoyable, it didn't fulfill her deepest desire to raise a family. The extra money she made helped pay some of their bills, but many expenses from her hospital stay hadn't yet been covered.

Doris had been enjoying a day off and was about to begin washing the breakfast dishes when she glanced out the kitchen window. She was surprised to see her brother's truck pull in. She hadn't heard from Joel in several weeks, and he'd even quit doing things to try and win the right to open his envelope. She hadn't been able to figure that out because, until then, he'd been so open about how much he needed money.

We all need money, Doris thought as she dried her hands on a clean towel. *Arlene and Larry have expenses, and John and Elsie need to build a new house. There is no doubt in my mind that a large sum of money is in Dad's bank account. But thanks to Joel, none of us can touch a penny of it.*

She waited until Joel got out of

his truck, then went to the door to greet him. The minute he stepped onto the porch, Doris knew there was something different about her brother. Gone were the worry lines on his forehead and dark circles beneath his eyes. There was no grim twist to his mouth, nor the determined swagger he normally had. Instead, Joel's countenance was serene, as he smiled and took Doris's hand. Speaking in a gentle, sincere tone, he said, "I have something for you. It should help your current financial situation." He reached into his jacket pocket, pulled out an envelope, and handed it to her.

"What's this?" she questioned.

"Open it and see."

Doris did as he asked. Staring at the certified check inside, all she could do at first was manage a little squeak. "One hundred thousand dollars? Where did you get this kind of money, Joel, and why are you giving it to me?"

He gestured to the door. "Let's go inside, and I'll explain."

When they entered the living room, Doris called for Brian, who'd been in the bathroom, brushing his teeth. After he joined them, they all took a seat, and Doris showed him the check Joel had given her.

Brian's eyes narrowed as he looked at Joel with disbelief. "What's this all about?"

"I sold a very expensive classic car I got at an auction several months ago," Joel explained. "I was able to get top dollar for it, and this is one-third of the money. Arlene and Elsie will each get a third as well. I'll be going to see them after I leave here."

Doris sat on the sofa with her hands folded in her lap, unable to take it all in. "But why, Joel? What made you sell the car?" She scooted to the edge of her seat.

Joel's eyes watered, and his chin quivered slightly as he began speaking. "On a cold night in February, when thunder sounded during a snowstorm, I thought about Dad and all the things I'd done to hurt him, as well as the rest of my family." His voice cracked, and he paused to pull a hankie from his pocket. "I read some verses in the Bible Kristi had given me last Christmas, and it opened my eyes to the truth. I've been selfish and arrogant. Because of it, I've lost Kristi — the love of my life. Dad died without ever knowing that I loved him." He looked at Doris with pleading eyes. "Can you forgive me for being so self-centered?"

Doris's heart went out to her brother. She knew without reservation that his apology was heartfelt. She was certain he hadn't sold his car and given her the check so he could receive his share of Dad's estate. Joel's trembling shoulders and the sadness in his eyes let her know he was truly repentant.

She went over to him quickly and

gave him a hug. "I forgive you, Joel. And if Dad were here right now, he would forgive you, too. He only wanted the best for you and all his children."

"I believe you're right." Joel swiped at the tears that had escaped his eyes.

Doris looked at Brian, hoping he would say something, but he sat quietly, staring at the floor. After several seconds, he turned to Joel and said, "We appreciate your gesture, and it's good that you've seen the error of your ways. However, we can't take the check."

The color drained from Joel's face. "Why not? It's a gift — no strings attached."

Brian tipped his head. "Seriously?

You don't expect anything in return?"

Joel shook his head briskly, making a sweeping movement with his hand. "Nothing at all. I don't care about Dad's money anymore."

Shocked by this admission, Doris hugged him again. "You really have changed, haven't you? It was all in the Lord's timing."

"Yes, and my eyes have been opened. I have a lot of things to make up for, and this is only the beginning."

She smiled. "If you need our help in any way, don't hesitate to ask."

Joel nodded. "I need to finish saying what's on my heart."

"Certainly. Go ahead."

"In addition to giving you, Elsie,

and Arlene the money from the sale of my car, I plan to help build a new home for Elsie and John." Joel drew in a deep breath and exhaled slowly. "I'm also going to start spending more time with my family and be there whenever they need me."

Doris's eyes filled with joyful tears. Joel might not be living among them anymore, but she felt as if he'd truly come home.

Farmerstown

When Joel pulled into Arlene's yard and got out of his truck, he was greeted by Scott playing in the yard with his dog.

"Hey, Uncle Joel, I'm glad you're here. Would ya like to see some of the tricks I've taught Bristleface?"

Joel ruffled the boy's hair. "Maybe in a little bit. Right now, I need to speak to your *mamm* and daed. Are they both here?"

"Mom is, but my dad took Doug to the Shoe and Boot store in Charm. My bruder's *fiess* have grown so much his toes are about to poke through his shoes."

"Maybe he'll have big feet like mine." Smiling, Joel lifted one foot. "When I was a teenager, my daed used to say I had clodhoppers."

Scott snickered. "Never heard that expression before."

Joel glanced toward the house, then back at his nephew. "I'm going inside to talk to your mamm right now, but I'll be back soon.

Then you can show me all the tricks you've taught your hund."

"Okay!" Scott gave the edge of Joel's jacket a tug. "Oh, and guess what else?"

"What?"

"I've been practicin' the harmonica every chance I get. I can play a couple of tunes pretty good."

"That's great. I'll be anxious to hear what you've learned." Joel bent down to give the dog's head a quick pat. "After you've shown me what this scruffy little terrier can do, we'll sit on the porch awhile, and you can play your tunes."

"Ya mean you don't have to rush off?" Scott knelt, and Bristleface plopped down next to him.

"Not today, Scott. For that matter, I plan to come around here more often and get to know you and my other nephews and nieces a lot better."

The boy's eyes widened, and a big grin spread across his face. "Really, Uncle Joel?"

"Jah, that's right." As Joel turned and stepped onto the porch, he smiled. He'd missed so much by not spending time with his family, but that was all behind him now.

When Joel walked into Arlene's kitchen and handed her a check for her portion of the car sale, she was so surprised she had to sit down at the table. "Where did you come up with this much money, and why are you giving it to me?"

"It's one-third of what I made selling the fancy Corvette I bought some time ago." He took a seat in the chair beside her. "I've always wanted a car like that, and until recently, I had no intention of ever letting it go. I kept it a secret — from my family, as well as Kristi, which was wrong."

"What changed your mind? Was it because you needed money and haven't been able to get your hands on Dad's?" Arlene's tone was bitter, and she bit her tongue to keep from saying more.

"The money's not for me. I divided it three ways between you, Doris, and Elsie."

She stared at the check. "Do my sisters know about this?"

"Only Doris so far. I'll be going to see Elsie next, to give her —"

"Give me what?" Elsie asked, entering the room.

Arlene's eyes widened as she turned to look at her sister. "I knew you were coming over today to help me do some cleaning but didn't realize you were here already."

"I just arrived." Elsie moved closer to the table. "What is it you planned to give me, Joel — another gift to try and sway me to say you've done something selfless?" She removed her sweater and hung it over the back of the chair next to her.

"It's nothing like that." He motioned for her to sit down, then reached into his pocket and handed her a check.

Elsie's mouth formed an *O*. "One hundred thousand dollars? What's this all about, Joel?"

Speaking calmly, he explained about the fancy car he'd sold and how he'd divided the money three ways.

Elsie glanced at Arlene, then back at Joel. "Is this another attempt at getting your share of the inheritance?"

He shook his head. "Through the reading of some scripture, plus a lot of soul-searching and praying, I've committed my life to the Lord. I realize how selfish I've been all these years, and I want to make amends." Joel paused and clasped his sisters' hands. "I can't begin to tell you both how sorry I am for all the hurtful things I've done in the past. But it's going to be different from now on, starting with this money I'm giving you. I expect nothing in return — no strings attached, like I said to Doris and Brian a while ago. I don't care anymore about whatever Dad wanted me to have."

"Are you *anscht*?" Arlene could hardly believe the things Joel said. He'd been living for himself so long, with no regard for any of them, it was hard to accept that he could have changed. But the Bible was true, and lives were transformed when people accepted it and put God's principles into practice. If Joel truly had surrendered his life to Christ, then the slate was wiped clean, and he could begin anew.

"I'm very serious." Joel's eyes filled with tears. "Will you both forgive me?"

Arlene looked at Elsie, and when she nodded, they spoke at the same time. "I forgive you, Joel."

"My change of heart and repentance goes beyond the money I gave you both," he said. "Elsie, as you know, I make my living building and remodeling, and I plan to help as much as I can with rebuilding a house for you and your family."

Elsie's eyes clouded as she squeezed Joel's hand. "Danki. Your help will be most appreciated."

He looked at Arlene and smiled. "From now on, I want to spend more time with everyone in my family. Will that be all right with you?"

"It's more than all right." A sob caught in her throat. *Thank You, God. Joel's become the brother I've always longed for, and I feel sure he's truly had a change of heart.*

Chapter 8

Charm

The next Monday, Arlene and her sisters got together in the evening to talk about Joel.

"I think our bruder was sincere when he gave us those checks," Arlene said as the three of them sat at the kitchen table in Dad's old house. "He seemed genuinely repentant for neglecting all of us, too."

"I agree. I've never seen Joel with such a peaceful expression as he

153

had when he visited us on Saturday." Elsie went to the refrigerator and took out the Millionaire Pie she'd made. After slicing it and placing the pan on the table, she passed some plates to her sisters.

Doris smiled and took a piece. "Yum. This is one of my favorite pies."

"Mine, too," Arlene agreed.

"Getting back to Joel, when he came by to see me and Brian, I noticed right away how different he looked. He even spoke in a softer tone," Doris said. "I think we should call Aunt Verna and let her know what's happened. It's time for us to take a vote."

Arlene nodded. "I already know what my vote will be."

Elsie pushed her chair aside and stood. "I'll go out to the phone shack right now and give her a call. The sooner we get this settled, the better it will be for all of us."

The following day, Elsie was dusting the living-room furniture when she heard a car pull into the yard. Going to the door, she was surprised to see Aunt Verna getting out of a van. The lady driver got out, opened the back hatch, and lifted out a suitcase, placing it on the ground.

Aunt Verna reached for the handle and began to tug the suitcase along the ground.

Elsie wrapped her woolen shawl around her shoulders and rushed outside. Walking carefully around the piles of snow still in the yard, she saw Aunt Verna let go of the handle, then she greeted her with a hug. "I'm surprised to see you so soon. When we spoke yesterday, you said you'd try to be here by the end of the week."

The elderly woman tipped her head. "What was that?"

Speaking louder, Elsie repeated what she'd said.

Aunt Verna smiled and patted Elsie's shoulder. "My driver has other plans for the end of the week. Since she was only available today and tomorrow, I decided I'd better come now. I would have called first, but I wasn't sure when you would check your messages, so I decided to just come ahead."

"Well, I'm glad you're here. I'll try calling Doris and Arlene, but I don't know if I can reach them today."

"That's okay. I can stay till tomorrow evening. That's when my driver will be back to pick me up."

While Aunt Verna said goodbye to her driver, Elsie bent down and picked up her small suitcase. *No sense trying to pull this travel bag through piles of snow.* Out of consideration for her aunt, she would put her things in the downstairs bedroom, and she and John would sleep upstairs. That meant Glen and Blaine would have to share a room again, but it was only for one night, so it shouldn't be a problem.

Once inside, Elsie took her aunt's coat and other outer garments and hung them up. "Have you had lunch yet?"

"Do I have a hunch about what?"

"No, I asked if you've had lunch yet. I've eaten already, but there's some leftover *schplittaerbs supp* I can reheat if you want."

Aunt Verna's nose wrinkled. "I've never cared much for split-pea soup. Your daed always liked it, but not me."

"Oh, I see. Can I fix you a sandwich then?"

"No, it's okay. I developed a *koppweh* on the drive here and would really like to lie down awhile." She rubbed her temples.

"I'm sorry you have a headache.

I'll put your things in mine and John's room, and you can rest there on our bed." Elsie made sure to speak slowly and loud enough for her aunt to hear.

"Are you sure? I can take one of the bedrooms upstairs."

"The downstairs bedroom will be best. It'll be easier if you don't have to climb the stairs."

"Okay, if you insist. Elsie, could you please bring me a cold washcloth for my forehead?" Aunt Verna questioned before starting down the hall in the direction of the bedroom.

"Sure, no problem. I'll bring you a cup of chamomile tea and some aspirin, too," Elsie called.

Apparently her aunt didn't hear

what she said, for she continued down the hall without a response.

I'll take it to her anyway, Elsie thought as she started for the kitchen. *Then I'll go out to the phone shack and call Doris, Arlene, and Joel. Maybe we can all meet to talk about opening those envelopes before we sit down to a nice meal at the get-together this evening.*

Akron

As Joel headed down the freeway, he glanced in the rearview mirror and smiled. He didn't know why Elsie had invited him to join her family for supper this evening, but he'd gladly accepted the invitation. Besides enjoying a delicious home-cooked meal, he looked forward to spending time with her family.

He glanced at the satchel on the seat beside him, where he'd put his harmonica, then looked quickly back at the road. After they ate, he looked forward to playing a few tunes for the family. *Sure wish Arlene and her family could be there. I'll bet Scott would enjoy playing his harmonica with me.* The boy reminded Joel of himself at that age — full of curiosity and eager to try new things. *Sure hope he doesn't rebel like I did when he starts his running-around years. If he does, I'll speak up and try to guide him in the right direction.*

Joel winced, feeling a stab of regret. His parents and sisters — especially Doris — had tried to make him see the error of his ways, but he'd ignored them and done his own thing.

I wonder how things would be for me now if I hadn't rebelled. He gripped the steering wheel as a car passed him, going much too fast. *If I'd stayed Amish, I wouldn't have met Kristi. Maybe I was meant to be with Anna, but of course, I botched that up, too.*

Joel thought about the choices people made and how one simple act or decision could change the course of a person's life. His decision to go English had certainly set his life on a different path. If he'd remained Amish, he wouldn't have been so desperate to make money so he could acquire worldly things.

It wasn't that modern things were all bad, but putting material possessions ahead of family and always striving for more made people selfish and greedy. He wondered if his desire to own the Corvette had been purely to make him feel good about himself. When Joel had been out driving the car and people admired it, he'd felt proud of himself for owning something so nice — something the average person couldn't afford.

He didn't care about that anymore. He wanted to live a normal life, make a decent living, and someday find a sweet, Christian wife. *I almost did,* he reminded himself. *But she's out of my life now, and I need to quit dwelling on it.*

God's given me another chance, so I have to keep my focus on living a life pleasing to Him.

Charm

Joel stepped onto his dad's porch and was surprised when Aunt Verna opened the door. "I sure didn't expect to see you here this evening." He gave her a hug.

"I arrived this afternoon." She opened the door wider and let him in. "After you hang up your jacket, join me in the living room, where your sisters are waiting." She patted his shoulder.

Joel was even more surprised. When he'd received Elsie's invitation for supper, he'd assumed it would only be him and her family.

Having the rest of his family to-gether this evening would be even nicer, though. He looked forward to more gatherings like this.

Coming into his father's house and looking around, he felt differ-ent on the inside — better. *I'm sure my daed would be pleased to know that the stipulation he put in his will helped me pull out of a downward spiral.*

Bringing his thoughts to a halt, Joel placed his jacket on a wall peg and entered the living room, where Arlene, Doris, and Elsie sat on the couch. They were talking about Aunt Verna getting some new hear-ing aids. His sisters sounded thrilled, and his aunt said she couldn't wait to use them so she could hear like a kid again. There was no sign of his sisters' husbands, though, or any of their children.

"I'm glad you could make it, Joel. We'll eat supper after we've had our meeting." Elsie pointed to the recliner where Dad used to sit. "Please, take a seat."

He did as she'd requested, and Aunt Verna took a seat in the rocking chair.

"Where's everyone else?" Joel asked, looking around.

"The kinner are upstairs, and the men, including Glen and Blaine, are in the barn. They'll come inside as soon as we call them," Arlene replied.

Aunt Verna cleared her throat, before looking at Joel. "Your sisters have told me about the money you gave them from the sale of your fancy car."

He nodded.

"They also said you've had a change of heart and apologized for all the hurts you have caused your family." She kept her gaze steadily on him.

Joel rubbed the bridge of his nose, hoping he wouldn't break down. He still felt deep remorse for all the things he'd done in the past. "I made my peace with God, Aunt Verna. I've committed my life to Him and want to do things better from now on." He glanced at his sisters, all looking intently at him. "When I gave out those checks, I didn't expect anything in return.

And if I don't get anything from Dad's estate, that's okay, too."

"Did I hear you right, Joel?" Aunt Verna tipped her head, peering at him over the top of her glasses. "Did you just say if you didn't get anything from your daed's estate, it would be okay?"

"That's right." Joel dropped his gaze to the floor. "I treated Dad badly and don't deserve a single thing."

"But he wanted all of you to have something." Aunt Verna picked up four envelopes that had been lying on the small table to her left. "Your sisters and I have agreed that by selling your prized car and giving all the money to them, you've done a heartfelt, selfless act. Therefore, it's time for all of you to open your envelopes." She rose from her chair and handed each of them an envelope.

Joel looked at the one with his name on it, and his eyes filled with tears. All these months he'd been desperate to receive his inheritance, and now he hesitated to open the envelope. Maybe Dad hadn't left him anything at all. Or perhaps he'd given him equal shares in the money he'd made from the oil wells on his land. Whatever he got of monetary value, Joel didn't feel deserving of it.

With trembling fingers, he opened the envelope and read the note inside: "To my son, Joel, I leave my house, the barn, and the three acres the two buildings sit on." Joel was fully aware that the rest of Dad's acreage was where the oil wells sat, so he wouldn't get any profit from those. And there had been no mention of Joel getting any of the money in Dad's bank account, which meant, with the exception of the horses in the barn, and the house he'd grown up in, Joel hadn't been given anything of real value.

Joel clasped his hands together in his lap. *Guess I'm getting exactly what I deserve. Sure don't know what I'm gonna do with the barn or house.*

CHAPTER 9

Berlin

On the first Saturday of April, another day off for Doris, she'd gone to town to run a few errands. It was nice to know their financial burdens would be lifted soon. Now they wouldn't have to be stressed out, trying to make ends meet. Doris needed to consider whether she wanted to continue working or stay home and keep house.

Her last stop before heading home was the pharmacy inside the

German Village complex. As she approached the cashier with her purchases, she glanced to the left and saw Kristi Palmer heading her way.

"It's so nice to see you, Doris." Kristi smiled, toting some bottles of vitamins. "It's been awhile since we talked, and I've been wondering how you and your family are doing."

"A lot has happened since we last spoke. If you have a few minutes, maybe we can sit on a bench outside the store and visit."

"I have plenty of time. I just came from the quilt shop where I went to buy material for the queen-sized quilt I'm making." Kristi set her purchases on the counter and opened the satchel she'd been carrying over her shoulder. "Here, let me show you the color of materials I picked for my quilt." She opened the bag and pulled up the fabric.

"Oh, those shades of purple are so pretty." Doris paused until Kristi put the material back in place. "I didn't realize you knew how to quilt."

"I didn't — not until I took some classes from the Amish lady at the quilt shop on Main Street." Kristi picked up her vitamins and got in line behind Doris. "When you gave me that beautiful wall hanging I became inspired."

"Do you still have it?" Doris turned and looked at her intently.

"Definitely. It's hanging on my

bedroom wall. I think it looks great there, and it has a special meaning for me."

Doris was pleased to hear this. She half-expected Kristi to get rid of the quilted piece after her breakup with Joel.

When they'd paid for their purchases, Doris led the way out of the store, where she found an empty bench near the Christian bookstore. After they'd both taken a seat, she filled Kristi in on all that had happened since their last visit, including the fire that destroyed Elsie and John's house, as well as what Joel had done with the money from the sale of his classic car.

Kristi looked at Doris in disbelief. "Did he do it so he could get his inheritance?"

"No. In fact, Joel said he didn't care about the money anymore. He just wanted —"

An elderly Amish woman came up to Doris and rested her hand on the back of the bench. "Do you know whether your sister Elsie is home today?"

"I'm not sure," Doris replied. "Is there something you need to ask her?"

The woman smiled. "I wanted to let her know that my son Harold is available to help when they're ready to move into their new house."

"It's nice of him to offer, Ada. They'll be moving out of Dad's old place the last Saturday of this month, so I'm sure they'll appreciate all the help they can get."

"I'll let Harold know." Ada said goodbye and headed into the market across the way.

Doris turned to face Kristi. "I'm sorry. I should have introduced you. Ada's been a friend of our family for years. In fact, she used to go to school with my dad."

"It's all right. I wasn't offended." Kristi held her purse in her lap, twisting the strap around her fingers. "I'm really sorry to hear about Elsie losing her house. Is there anything they need?"

"Furniture, mostly, but now that my sisters and I will get our share of Dad's estate, Elsie will be able to afford whatever she needs."

"That's wonderful news." Kristi

stood. "I need to get going. It was nice seeing you, Doris. Please tell your sisters I said hello."

Doris rose from the bench and gave Kristi a hug. Then she picked up her things and headed toward her horse and buggy, which were secured at one of the hitching rails in the parking lot. She'd hoped Kristi might ask her to say hello to Joel, too. Apparently she didn't care about him anymore.

How sad, she thought when she turned and saw Kristi walk away. *She didn't even seem that interested when I tried to tell her Joel has changed. Maybe the relationship between Kristi and my brother was never meant to be.*

■ ■ ■ ■

When Kristi entered the Farmstead Restaurant and saw the long line that went almost out the door, she realized she'd probably have to wait awhile before being seated at a table. Since she wasn't in a hurry to get home, she didn't really mind the wait. Besides, it would give her a chance to digest all that Doris had told her. Was it possible Joel had actually changed? Could he really have sold his Corvette and given his sisters the money? For his family's sake, she hoped it was true.

It's a shame he couldn't have changed when we were still dating, Kristi thought. *It's been quite a while since I last heard from Joel. If he loved me, the way he said he did, I would think he'd have let me know he'd made things right with his family.* She shifted her purse to the other shoulder. *But then, I chose not to respond to any of the messages he did leave, so I guess it makes sense that he didn't call later.*

Kristi assumed that, more than six months after their breakup, Joel had moved on with his life. For her, though, it had been hard to move on — at least when it came to dating. She was actually thankful Darin hadn't pursued a relationship with her. She was content to be his friend.

It's still hard for me to fathom that Joel could have changed. I wonder what all he said to make Doris be-

lieve him. Could he have only said it to get his inheritance, or is it possible that — Kristi's thoughts halted when the person behind her nudged her arm gently. "Excuse me, Miss, but the people ahead of you have moved to the front of the line."

"Oh, sorry." Kristi's cheeks warmed as she quickly stepped forward. She was almost to the hostess's desk and could see into part of the restaurant, including the all-you-can-eat buffet. She watched the young Amish waitress clear a table, wiping the area clean as soon as the customers rose and headed for the desk to pay for their meal. Several other workers moved quickly about, trying to cater to many hungry patrons.

Her mouth watered, smelling the delicious aromas. She could hardly wait until it was her turn to be seated at a table. Kristi had eaten at this restaurant before and re-membered how good the baked chicken on the buffet had tasted. Another thing Kristi had enjoyed were the pickled red beets. *After I'm seated and it's time to place my order, I'm definitely going to do the buffet.*

Kristi didn't normally eat much for lunch, but today she'd make an exception and would probably be full the rest of the day. *I may not have to eat any supper tonight, but if I get hungry later, I'll fix a light snack. I probably should go for a run as soon as I get home, to burn off all the calories I'll be eating today.*

The man and woman in front of Kristi were being seated, so it was her turn next. Her stomach growled, and she placed her hand over it, hoping no one had heard. In a short while she'd be choosing whatever she wanted from the delicious array of foods on the buffet.

Looking to the right, where a man and woman sat in a booth, Kristi's breath caught in her throat. It was Joel, with the pretty Amish woman she'd seen him talking to the day of his father's funeral. When she'd asked Joel about it later, he'd said the woman's name was Anna, and that he'd been engaged to marry her before he left the Amish faith.

Apparently they were back together, for Joel reached across the table and placed his hand on Anna's.

I can't believe it. Unbidden tears sprang to Kristi's eyes. *I should have expected he would eventually give up on me. No wonder Joel hasn't called or left any messages for so long. He's obviously back with his old girlfriend.* A lump lodged in her throat. *I bet he's planning to return to the Amish faith again, too. Or maybe Joel's convinced Anna to become part of the English world with him.*

The hostess returned from seating the other people, but before she could say anything, Kristi turned, nearly bumping into the gentleman behind her, and rushed out the door. She'd waited all that time to be seated, but now her appetite was gone.

Joel smiled as Anna told him about Melvin Mast, who had recently started courting her. He couldn't remember ever seeing her face glow like this — not even when the two of them had been courting. Anna deserved to be happy, and he wished her well, reaching across the table and placing his hand over hers.

Joel hadn't made plans to meet Anna here for lunch. They'd both arrived around the same time, and after learning she was alone, he'd invited her to sit with him. He was anxious to see how she was doing and tell her that he'd committed his life to the Lord. Anna seemed as happy for Joel as he was for her starting a relationship with Melvin. They'd laughed and talked when they began eating, and Joel couldn't remember the last time he'd felt so relaxed in her presence. Of course, he felt better around everyone these days — especially his family members.

Joel thought about the inheritance he'd received from his father and bit back a chuckle. There would have been a day he'd have been hopping mad at Dad for leaving him so little and at his sisters for getting much more than him. Not that it was their fault. None of them knew what Dad had designated in his will. To Joel's surprise, shortly after Doris, Arlene, and Elsie opened their envelopes, they'd each offered to give him part of the money they'd been left. He'd said no. He didn't deserve one penny of what Dad wanted his daughters to have. All three of them had been dutiful to Dad — especially after Mom died and he'd needed their help. Joel's sisters had always been kind and loving to their parents; unlike him, who'd given Mom and Dad nothing but trouble and heartache.

Once more, Joel wished he could turn back the hands of time and begin again. Knowing what he did now, if he could start over, he'd be a better son and brother. Well, he couldn't undo the past, but he'd spend the rest of his days trying to make it up to his sisters and their families.

"Joel, did you hear what I said?" Anna's question drove his thoughts aside, and he blinked a couple of times. "Sorry, I was spacing — kind of lost in my thoughts."

"There's a young woman out by the hostess's desk, and she looks a lot like the woman you brought to your daed's funeral." Anna pointed in that direction.

He turned his head sharply, but only caught a glimpse of the back of a woman's auburn head as she hurried from the restaurant. "That couldn't have been Kristi," he murmured. "What would she be doing here?"

CHAPTER 10

Charm

"We need some more boxes to load up the last of your food items," Joel called to Elsie as he emptied one of the kitchen cupboards.

"I think there are some more in the barn." She smiled. "Thank you for taking the day off to help us move. We also appreciate all the work you've done on our new home."

"I was happy to do it, Elsie." Joel glanced around the kitchen. "Now

189

I need to figure out what to do with Dad's house."

She placed her hand on his arm. "It belongs to you now. For whatever reason, Dad wanted you to have it."

"I realize that, but I have my own place in Akron."

"You said it's a mobile home, right?"

He nodded.

Elsie made a sweeping gesture of the kitchen. "This isn't fancy, but it's a solidly built home. With the three acres it sits on, there'd be room for you to build a shop for all the tools and supplies you need for your construction business."

Joel massaged the back of his neck. "Are you suggesting I sell my place and move here?"

"It'd be nice for all of us if you did. Keeping the home we grew up in would be meaningful, and living closer would give us opportunities to see you more often."

He tilted his head, weighing his choices. He could either sell Dad's place and use the money to build a new house on the property he owned now, or sell his land and mobile home and move here. If he did the latter, he'd have to update the house, connect to the power lines, and get an Internet provider, because he needed that for his business and computer. Since the jobs Joel often did were in various locations, he didn't need to live in Akron. He could commute to most anywhere in this part of Ohio within a few hours' drive. Still, what would he do in this rambling old house all alone? If he had a wife and children, it would be a nice place to live and raise a family. But by himself, all he'd have were the memories from growing up here as a child.

"Are you thinking about my suggestion?" Elsie tugged on his shirtsleeve.

"I am, and as nice as it would be to live closer to you and the rest of our family, it may not be the sensible thing to do."

"Well, give it some thought before you make a final decision." Elsie looked at the open cupboard they'd just emptied of food.

"I will. And I'll be praying about it, too." Joel turned toward the back door. "I'll head out to the barn now and look for those boxes."

Elsie grabbed a sponge and rinsed it in the sink; then she stepped over to the cupboard and started wiping the shelves. "Okay. If you see Aunt Verna, would you let her know I could use her help in here? She went outside some time ago to hang a few dishtowels on the line, and I haven't seen her since."

He chuckled. "You know our dear aunt. She can easily become distracted."

"You're right about that. It was nice of her and Uncle Lester to come down to help with the move." Elsie grinned. "I think she's looking forward to spending the next few nights in our new home. Since it has two bedrooms on the main floor, she and Uncle Lester can have a cozy room on the first floor, and John and I won't have to give up our room."

"They could stay here, you know."

"Right, but since Glen will be staying here until you decide what to do with the place, I thought he would enjoy having some peace and quiet without any visitors."

Joel gave his sister a hug. "You're a thoughtful *mudder.*" He opened the back door and stepped out.

Grinning, Aunt Verna waved at him from where she was rocking back and forth on the porch swing.

He smiled in response. "I can see

you're enjoying yourself. But when you get tired of swinging, Elsie could you use your help in the kitchen."

Her forehead wrinkled. "Elsie has a kitten?"

Joel resisted the urge to laugh. *She must not have her new hearing aids turned on.* "No, she said she needs your help in the kitchen."

"Oh, of course." She rose from the swing, pausing for a minute to watch some robins searching for worms in the grass, before going into the house.

Joel headed for the barn. He'd barely set foot inside when Dad's spirited horse started acting up, kicking at the back wall in his stall. *I wonder what's got him so worked up.*

Speaking softly to the horse, Joel entered the stall. "Whoa, boy. Settle down."

With an ear-piercing whinny, the horse reared up, then kicked again — this time putting a hole in the wall.

Joel figured a cat, or even a mouse, may have spooked the horse. He grabbed a rope, put it around the animal's neck, and tied him to the other side of the stall. Then he knelt in front of the wall to examine the damage. When Joel peered into the gaping hole, he was surprised to see something shiny. It looked like a piece of chrome, but it wasn't close enough for him to reach. The horse's stall was at the back of the barn, where outside, dirt was built up along the whole side and stretched out into the hillside. Dad had called it a "bank barn." Joel used to climb up on the mound of dirt when he was a boy and pretend he was standing on a mountain. He remembered once, Dad had caught him playing up there and told him in no uncertain terms to get off and never go up there again. When Joel asked why, Dad said, "Because you could fall and get hurt." Joel never understood what the big deal was. The mound of dirt wasn't that high. But he'd done as Dad asked and never went near it again. For that matter, Dad had been fussy about Joel or anyone else coming into this particular stall. Joel always figured it was because Dad had been so finicky about his own horse.

Gazing back at the hole, Joel decided to investigate further. He was curious about what was behind the wall. "Better get a flashlight," he mumbled.

After moving the horse to another stall, Joel was about to head out to his truck when he spotted a flashlight on the shelf halfway up the wall. Several shelves made the wall inside the stall look like a huge, built-in bookcase that went from top to bottom and all the way from one side to the other along the back wall.

Reaching up to get the flashlight, Joel touched something cold. It felt like a knob. Twisting it to the left, he was stunned when the bookcase-like structure swung open, revealing another room, apparently hidden under all the dirt behind the barn.

"What in the world?" Joel turned the flashlight on and shined the beam of light into the room. His nose twitched when he stepped inside. The room had a different smell. Dust, mixed with fuel and rubber, tainted the air.

He rested his hands on his hips. "What did Dad keep secret in here?"

Seeing a lot of things covered with tarps, he moved to the closest one and pulled it back. A beautiful old car came into view.

"Oh, wow!" Like a kid in a candy store, Joel went to each tarp, pulling them off. It seemed like a dream, but he'd just discovered not one, but ten antique classic cars hidden under all those dusty tarps.

Joel's breath caught in his throat. "I'll bet these beauties are worth millions!"

Yelling for Elsie, he dashed out of the barn.

Humming to the tune of the song playing on her car radio, Kristi turned off the freeway in the direction of Charm. She wasn't sure if Elsie and her family still lived in Eustace's old house, but she had something for them and hoped to deliver it today. If they had already moved to their new home, then Kristi didn't know what to do, because she did not have their new address.

"I should have thought to ask Doris," Kristi muttered. She would have liked to have brought this love gift sooner, but it had taken a few weeks for donations to come in after she'd gotten the word out to church members about the fire that had destroyed the home of Joel's sister. Even though Doris had said she and her siblings would receive an inheritance from their father, Kristi didn't know how much it was or whether they'd gotten the money yet. She wanted to do something to help out. In addition to several boxes of food, the church had collected over a thousand dollars in cash. It wasn't an enormous amount of money, but it would help with some of their expenses. Kristi felt grateful for the congregation's generosity to a family they'd never met.

That's what all churches should do, she thought, turning on the road that led to Eustace Byler's house. *Helping people in need, regardless of whether we know them or not, is the Christian thing to do, and it's a testimony of Christ's love for us.*

When she pulled into the yard a few minutes later, Kristi noticed a teenage Amish boy wearing a straw hat, carrying a cardboard box over to a truck parked near the house. Her heart began to pound — it was the truck Joel used for work, which meant he must be here. From the looks of the boxes stacked on the front porch, this must be moving day for Elsie's family. As much as she dreaded facing Joel, Kristi wasn't leaving here until she'd seen Elsie and given her the church's gifts.

Turning off the engine, she stepped out of the car. When she approached the young man, she asked if Elsie was there.

He pointed to the barn. "Joel's there, too — looking at the new cars he just got. He says they're worth a whole lot of money, so now Uncle Joel has a big collection of cars." The boy bobbed his head, grinning widely. "My uncle is rich!"

Kristi's spine stiffened. Apparently Joel had not changed at all. His emphasis was still on money, and now he'd bought more cars. *Won't he ever get his priorities right?*

"Would you please get your mother?" she asked. "I have some things in the car I want to give her." With any luck, only Elsie would come out, and she'd avoid seeing Joel at all.

The boy nodded and headed for the barn. A few minutes later, Elsie appeared . . . and Joel was with her.

Joel halted when he stepped out of the barn and saw Kristi standing beside her car. He had no idea what she was doing here, but the sight of her beautiful face and auburn hair made his heart race. If he hadn't known she had a new boyfriend, he would have dashed over to her, explained that he'd become a Christian, and begged her once again to take him back. He'd never loved another woman the way he did her. Even though he didn't deserve a second chance, if Kristi would forgive Joel for his past mistakes and agree to become his wife, he'd spend the rest of his life trying to make her happy.

Heart thumping so hard blood pulsated in his head, Joel approached Kristi. Before he had a chance to say anything, she smiled at Elsie and said, "Doris told me about your house burning down, and I've brought you a little something from my church." She opened her trunk and pointed to several boxes full of food. Then she reached into her purse, pulled out an envelope, and handed it to Elsie. "Please accept this love gift and use it in any way you need for your new home."

"I . . . I don't know what to say." Elsie's eyes filled with tears. "Thanks to the inheritance I've received from my dad, my husband and I have all the money we need, so I don't feel right about taking this."

Kristi glanced briefly at Joel, then looked quickly back at Elsie. "I would like you to have it. I'm sure you can use the extra food, and if you don't need the money, feel free to pass it along to someone else in need."

"That's called 'paying it forward,' " Joel spoke up.

Without looking at him, Kristi nodded.

Elsie hugged Kristi. "Please tell your church people I said thank you." She gave Joel's arm a little nudge. "I'll leave you two alone so you can talk. I believe you have some catching up to do." Without another word, she hurried into the house. Joel's nephew removed one of the boxes from Kristi's truck and followed his mother inside.

Palms sweaty and heart still beating hard, Joel cleared his throat. "Umm . . .there's something I'd like you to know, Kristi."

"Don't tell me. Let me guess. You've gotten a huge inheritance from your dad, so you've purchased several more cars, which you are keeping in his barn."

He shook his head vigorously. "No, it's not like that."

Her eyes narrowed. "How is it then?"

Joel quickly explained how he'd accidentally found the secret room in his dad's barn, and was surprised to find the old cars. "At first I couldn't figure out why they were there or how they even got in the hidden room behind the barn." He paused and drew in a quick breath. "Then my aunt came out, and after I showed her what I'd found, she informed me that a long time ago, when Dad was a teenager, he'd had his own car. It was during his running-around years, when he'd been allowed to experience some things outside the Amish world."

Kristi stared at him with an uncertain expression.

"Anyway," Joel continued, "Aunt Verna said even after Dad sold his car and joined the church, he often talked about his interest in classic cars. Nobody had any idea his interest went further than merely talking about cars." He motioned to the barn, slowly shaking his head. "Apparently over the years, Dad bought several old cars and snuck them in a room behind a secret door. So now . . ."

"I know — your nephew told me

— you're rich."

Joel pulled his fingers through his thick hair. "If I sell them, I probably will get a lot of money, but I won't keep it all. I'll give a good chunk of it to someone in need." He took a step closer to her. "You see, Kristi, after committing my life to God, I've come to realize how selfish I was, and I've changed."

"He's telling you the truth," Aunt Verna said when she came out of the barn.

Joel was surprised his aunt had even heard what he'd said, but then he remembered her new hearing aids and figured she'd finally turned them on.

Aunt Verna stepped up to them and placed both hands on Kristi's shoulders. "My nephew is not the same person he was before. He sold his first classic car to help his family, and now, thanks to my brother's will stating that Joel should have the house, barn, and everything in it, he has more cars to sell so he can help others."

Joel gave his aunt a quick wink. "If no one has any objections, I may keep one of the cars. It'll be fun to fix it up. Then every time I drive it, I'll think of Dad."

"I think that would be fine, Joel." Aunt Verna slipped her arm around his waist. "Your daed was a bit eccentric, which is probably why he bought all those vehicles when he knew it went against our church rules for a member to own a car.

But given that he kept them in the secret room for his own amusement and didn't drive them, I'm sure if anyone outside our family hears of this, they'll understand."

"I hope so, but even if they don't, what's done is done. We can't go back and change the past."

"No, but we can make the best of the here and now and plan well for our future." Aunt Verna stepped aside and gave Joel a gentle push toward Kristi. "You two are obviously in love with each other. Don't you think you ought to talk things through and begin again?"

Before either Joel or Kristi could respond, his aunt turned and headed for the house.

Trembling for fear of her rejection, Joel looked directly at Kristi. "Aunt Verna's right. I do still love you, but I won't try to get in the way of your new relationship."

Her forehead wrinkled. "What new relationship?"

Joel explained about the day he'd shown up at church and seen her sitting beside a blond-haired man.

"That was Darin, our new youth pastor." Kristi shook her head. "We're not in a relationship. We're just friends."

Joel heaved a sigh of relief.

"But aren't you in a relationship, Joel?"

"What makes you think that?"

"I saw you at the Farmstead Restaurant in Berlin a few weeks ago with the young woman you used to date. You were holding her hand."

So it was Kristi I saw leaving the restaurant that day. Laughter bubbled in Joel's chest and spilled over.

She tipped her head. "What's so funny?"

"Anna and I aren't back together. We ran into each other by accident that day and decided to share a table. I wasn't holding her hand, either. I only touched it when I was telling her I was glad to hear she's being courted by a new man in her church district."

Kristi's cheeks flamed a bright pink. "So we both assumed the other was seeing someone else, when neither of us has ever gotten over the other."

He reached for her hand and was glad when she didn't pull it away. "Does that mean you still love me?"

She nodded slowly. "I've tried to fight it and denied my feelings so many times I began to believe it was true. But the day I saw you with Anna, I knew the love I felt for you had never really died."

Joel smiled with relief. "Can you ever forgive me for all the hurt I caused? Would you be willing to give me another chance?"

"Yes," she murmured, tears shimmering in her eyes.

Barely able to speak around the lump lodged in his throat, Joel dropped to his knees. "Kristi Palmer, would you do me the honor of becoming my wife?"

"I will."

Joel stood and pulled Kristi into his arms. Hoping no one was watching their display of affection, he kissed her gently on the lips. When the kiss ended, he smoothed Kristi's hair back from her face and whispered, "When I finally realized that true compassion is feeling someone else's pain and doing something about it, I wanted to do a heartfelt, selfless act and didn't care about getting anything in return. When we raise our own children someday, I hope we can teach them that."

Kristi pressed her head against his chest. "We will, Joel. That's a promise."

EPILOGUE

One Year Later

Kristi stood at the kitchen window, looking out at the flowers and trees in full bloom. After being married to Joel these past six months, and living here in his father's old house, she still felt as though she were living a dream. Residing in Amish country and becoming part of her husband's wonderful family had filled a place in Kristi's heart she'd always felt was missing. To add to her joy, she'd been taking classes to become a midwife to the Amish and other women in the area. A week ago, she'd had the privilege of assisting the midwife when her sister-in-law's baby boy was born. What a miracle it was that the Lord had given Doris a healthy pregnancy and a strong infant. She and Brian named their son Andrew Joel. He was a sweet little guy, and seeing him sleeping in Doris's arms made Kristi eager to start her own family with Joel.

She glanced around the spacious kitchen Joel had remodeled to suit their needs. It wasn't fancy by English standards, but he'd installed electricity and given Kristi two oversized ovens. She looked forward to entertaining here for years to come. This evening, Arlene, Elsie, Doris, and their families would be coming over for a potluck dinner. Since Akron wasn't far away, her folks had been invited, too.

Turning her gaze back to the window, Kristi spotted Joel filling one of their bird feeders. These days, when he wasn't working on some job site for his business, his energies were spent on getting things done around here. Tonight, as most evenings, they would leave their television set off and enjoy a delightful time with their families.

Joel might not be a member of the Amish church, but the love he'd shown for his family and, most of all, for God proved that he was

Amish in his heart.

She smiled, thinking about her husband's identity here in this community. Joel had become known as the Amish millionaire's son, who cared about people more than himself, and whose generosity had helped many.

Kristi closed her eyes and whispered a prayer. "Thank You, Lord, for teaching us by Your example to look for ways to perform selfless acts."

MILLIONAIRE PIE

Ingredients:
2 (9 inch) baked pie shells
2 cups powdered sugar, not sifted
1 stick butter, softened
1 egg
1/4 teaspoon salt
1/4 teaspoon vanilla
1 cup whipping cream
1 cup crushed pineapple, well-
  drained
1/2 cup pecans

Cream powdered sugar and butter

in mixing bowl. Add egg, salt, and vanilla. Mix until fluffy. Spread mixture in baked pie shells. In another bowl, whip cream until it forms stiff peaks. Blend in well-drained pineapple and nuts. Spoon whipped-cream mixture on top of pies and chill until ready to serve.

ABOUT THE AUTHORS

New York Times bestselling, award-winning author **Wanda E. Brunstetter** is one of the founders of the Amish fiction genre. Wanda's ancestors were part of the Anabaptist faith, and her novels are based on personal research intended to accurately portray the Amish way of life. Her books are well-read and trusted by many Amish, who credit her for giving readers a deeper understanding of the people and their customs. When Wanda visits her Amish friends, she finds herself drawn to their peaceful lifestyle, sincerity, and close family ties. Wanda enjoys photography, ventriloquism, gardening, birdwatching, beachcombing, and spending time with her family. She and her husband, Richard, have been blessed with two grown children, six grandchildren, and two great-grandchildren.

To learn more about Wanda, visit her website at www.wanda brunstetter.com.

Jean Brunstetter became fascinated with the Amish when she first went to Pennsylvania to visit her father-in-law's family. Since that time, Jean has become friends with several Amish families and enjoys writing about their way of life. She also likes to put some of the simple practices followed by the Amish into her daily routine. Jean lives in Washington State with her husband, Richard Jr., and their three children, but takes every opportunity to visit Amish communities in several states. In addition to writing, Jean enjoys boating, gardening, and spending time on the beach.